Cocktails

Other titles by David Vernon:

Skeptical — a handbook of pseudoscience and the paranormal, (ed, with Laycock, Brown and Groves), 1989

Having a Great Birth in Australia, (ed) 2005

Men at Birth, (ed) 2006

With Women: midwives' experiences — from shiftwork to caseload (ed), 2007

The Umbrella's Shade and other award-winning stories from the Stringybark Short Story Awards, (ed), 2011

Men at Birth (2nd Edition - revised) (ed), 2011

Birth Stories — real and inspiring accounts from Australian women, (ed), 2011

Our Name Wasn't Written — A Malta Memoir (1936-1942) (3rd edition), (ed), 2011

Between Heaven and Hell and other award-winning stories from the Stringybark Flash Fiction Award, (ed), 2011

A Visit from the Duchess and other award-winning stories from the Stringybark Speculative Fiction Award, (ed), 2011

The Bridge and other stories from the Stringybark Short Story Awards — Editor's Choice Edition, (ed), 2011

The Heat Wave of '76 and other award-winning stories from the Stringybark Erotic Fiction Award, (ed), 2011

Marngrook and other award-winning stories from the Stringybark Australian History Short Story Award, (ed), 2012

Into the Darkness — one young Australian airman's journey from Sydney to the deadly skies over Germany, 1939 - 1945, (ed), 2012

The Road Home and other award-winning stories from the Stringybark Short Story Award, (ed), 2012

Between the Sheets — seventeen short stories from the Stringybark Erotic Fiction Awards — Editor's Choice Edition, (ed), 2012

Yellow Pearl — eighteen short stories from the Stringybark Australia History Award — Editor's Choice Edition, (ed), 2012

Tainted Innocence and other award-winning stories from the Twisted Stringybark Short Story Award, (ed), 2012

The Seven Deadly Sins and other award-winning stroies from the Stringybark Seven Deadly Sins Short Fiction Award, (ed), 2012

Behind the Wattles and seventy-seven award-winning stories from the Stringybark Flash and Microfiction Awards, (ed), 2012

Fight or Flight — twenty award-winning stories from the Stringybark Young Adult Fiction Awards, (ed), 2013

The Very End of the Affair — twenty-seven award-winning short stories from the Stringybark Hunorous Fiction Award, (ed), 2013

Hitler Did It — twenty-two short stories from the Stringybark Short Story Awards, (ed), 2013

Valentine's Day — twenty-three award-winning stories from the Stringybark Erotic Fiction Awards, (ed), 2013

Stew and Sinkers — thirty award-winning stories from the Stringybark 'Times Past' Short Fiction Awards, (ed), 2013

Malicious Mysteries — twenty-two award-winning stories from the Stringybark Malicious Mystery Short Story Awards. (ed). 2014

Side by Side — twenty-three award-winning stories from the Stringybark Short Story Awards, (ed), 2014

A Tick Tock Heart — twenty-two award-winning stories from the Stringybark Future Times Award, (ed), 2014

Role of a Lifetime — twenty-five award-winning stories from the Twisted Stringybark Award, (ed), 2014

Cocktails

twenty-five award-winning
stories
from the
Stringybark Erotic Short Fiction
Award

Edited
by
David Vernon

Selected by
Tessa King, Arna Walker, Jamie Todling
and
David Vernon

Stringybark Publishing
Australia

Cocktails — twenty-five award-winning stories from the Stringybark Erotic Short Fiction Awards

Published by
Stringybark Publishing,
PO Box 851, Jamison Centre, ACT 2614, Australia

www.stringybarkstories.net

First published: January 2015
Copyright © This collection, David Vernon, 2015
Copyright © Individual stories, the authors, various.

All rights reserved. No part of this publication may be reproduced, stored in retrieval systems or transmitted in any form or by any means (electronic or mechanical, through reprography, digital transmission, recording or otherwise) without the prior written permission of the publisher.

These are works of fiction and unless otherwise made clear, those mentioned in these stories are fictional characters and do not relate to anyone living or dead.

NATIONAL LIBRARY CATALOGUING-IN-PUBLICATION DATA ENTRY
Cocktails: twenty-five award-winning stories from the Stringybark Erotic Short Story Awards / edited by David Vernon
Edition: 1st
ISBN   9780992575908 (pbk).
Subjects: Short stories, Australian — 21st Century
                  Erotic stories, Australian — 21st Century
                  Stringybark Short Story Awards
                  Literary prizes — Australia
Other Authors/Contributors:
                  Vernon, David Michael John 1965- editor
Dewey Number: A823.01

Cover photo: Thomas Hawk
Cover design: David Vernon, www.davidvernon.net
Illustrations: Frances Underwood
Printed in Australia on Sustainable Forest FSC Paper

Contents

Introduction   i

Mermaid — Josh Redman	1
No Regrets — Sorcha Ni Mhaolmhuaidh	7
Dark and Stormy — Danielle Chedid	12
Deep Dark Secret — Claire Martijn	17
Screaming Orgasm — Maria Bonar	22
Make Believe — Robin Storey	25
White Russian — Julie Davies	31
Lychee Martini — Dusty Lane	36
Water from the River Ganges — Rowena Michel	41
Kiss in the Dark — Adam Ipsen	46
Hangman's Blood — Maria Bonar	51
Hot Carl Msagro — Diana Thurbon	56
Satin Sheets — Michael Wilkinson	60
Soixante-Neuf — Julie Davies	66
In the Saddle — R.L. Phoenix	72
Red Lotus — Samira Wyld	77
The Vibrator — Derek Wayne	82
Harvey Wallbanger — Meg Main	88
Dusty Rose — Shane von Liger	93
The Buzzer — Bernadette Frances	97
Adios Motherfucker — Michelle Irwin	102
Snow Ball — Jim Baker	108
After Dark — Claire Martijn	113
Firefly — Michael Wilkinson	117
Japanese Slipper — Jen Proctor	122

The Stringybark Erotic Short Fiction Award 2014	126
Cocktail Recipes	127
About the Judges	135
Acknowledgements	136

Introduction
— David Vernon

This is Stringybark Publishing's fourth foray into publishing erotic fiction. Our other books, *The Heat Wave of '76* (2011), *Between the Sheets* (2012) and *Valentine's Day* (2013) were so successful that we couldn't neglect running another competition for this most difficult of writing genres.

There is always a very thin line between pornography and erotica and what one person finds erotic another will find pornographic. For just such a reason we were careful to use four judges to choose the stories in this anthology. Importantly we made the decision early on that all four judges did not have to be in agreement for a story to be selected — a simple majority of judges would do. This ensures that you will find in these pages some edgy tales as well as the more classical forms of erotica.

The title of this collection comes from the original competition theme, which was for a writer to submit a tale that had a title that was the name of a cocktail. A web search will show an enormous number of cocktail names and thus we felt this gave wide creative scope to our writers. We think that the stories presented here show great imagination.

On behalf of all the judges, I hope you enjoy these sensual, erotic and sexy tales. And as a bonus, why not make a cocktail or two and sip them while you share this collection with the love of your life. You will find the recipes at the end of the book. Enjoy!

David Vernon
Judge and Editor
"Stringybark Stories"
January 2015

Mermaid
— Josh Redman

It was a beach a child would draw: a band of unbroken cream, topped off with a turquoise sea and an azure sky without the slightest dust of cloud anywhere within its boundless reach. Even the rolling dunes that rose up behind us were in regimental rows with neatly-coiffed grass tops.
"Fancy a quick dip?" I asked her.
"It'll be cold," she told her book.
"Clothes off, race to the sea and back in no time."
"You mean skinny dipping?"
"We might not get another chance like this."
"That would definitely be cold."
"How about if I throw in an ice cream?"
"Where would you get an ice cream?"
"I saw a van back at the car park."
"I don't want him seeing us."
"There's a mountain range of dunes in the way."
She stuck a finger in to mark the page of her book and looked up. "So if I agree to a quick nude dip then I get an ice cream and you leave me in peace to read?"
"Yes."
She tugged at various bows and her bikini fell away like wrapping paper. I slid my shorts off over my ankles and took another glance about to check the coast was clear. "Last one in is a…"
"Is a you!" she said, jumping up and launching into a sprint towards the sea. I ran after her and entered the water behind her wake of splashing and squealing. She turned and sent a wave of water over me.
"It's freezing!" she said, laughing. "I told you it would be cold."
I waded over to grasp her in a shivering hug. "At least give me a kiss before you escape."
I could taste sea salt on her lips, but this was quickly eclipsed by the warmth of her tongue sliding over mine. She broke off and her hand dropped down to the waterline where the lapping waves had completely washed away my erection.

Cocktails

"I think a kiss is all you're up to right now," she said. "Race you back to the towels."

We stomped back up the sand. She slid a towel over herself and patted her legs and body dry. Spreading out the towel again, she rolled over onto her front and retrieved her book.

"So what's the book about?" I asked.

"Humans all become extinct and so the mythical creatures — the mermaids, centaurs, fauns and things — they all come out of hiding and try to live in the empty world left by people."

"Sounds cheery."

"If I were a mermaid, would you want me to be fish upper half or fish lower half?"

"A mermaid is fish below and woman on top."

"But if you could choose."

"You'd be a bit odd as a fish head with legs."

"It's a choice between love and sex. You either get my top half to hold and kiss, but no pussy or arse, or you get to fuck me, but have to stare at a fish head. So, love or sex?"

"I love… having sex with you."

"That's a very male statement."

"And I have mad sex with you because I'm madly in love with you."

"That's better."

"Plus, I still get to play with your tits and the only sex we could have would be blow jobs, so it wouldn't be so bad."

"Blow jobs? A merman is a fish down below too."

"I was seeing myself as a hapless sailor who falls overboard and gets ravaged by a hot mermaid in his last few minutes."

"Aren't you supposed to be getting some ice creams?"

Returning with two ice cream cones, complete with chocolate flakes, I found her still on the beach naked. I passed her one of the cones.

Lying sideways next to her, I caressed her back and moved down to knead the cheeks of her arse. "You look quite comfy."

"No one's around," she said.

"I was thinking while walking back that maybe I could be a centaur. I still have a cock then."

"Your giant centaur love stick isn't going to fit in either end of a

Cocktails

mermaid. And if you think I'd let you shoot a horse's load anywhere near my mouth then you need to think again."

"I'd have to be a minotaur then."

"I don't fancy kissing a bull. You stick to being a centaur then and I'll become a sphinx."

"Then I lose your entire body and just have your head."

"Is my head not pretty enough?"

"I'd miss all the other bits."

"You can't get more pussy than a sphinx."

Having finished my ice cream, just the chocolate flake was sat in my mouth like a cigar. I pulled a camera from our bags and leant back to take a photo of her reading. She turned to stick her tongue out and then smiled for a follow up shot. I knelt up and took a snap from above her and then lay down the other way round to photograph her arse.

"Spread your legs a second," I said. "If you're going to turn into a sphinx then I need to document you so I can remember."

Without saying a word, her thighs parted and she swayed her feet side-to-side in rhythm with something she was reading. I took a few shots of her butt and between her legs and then put the camera down on the towel.

My hand slid between her cheeks and followed the cleft down until I felt her pussy wrap around my fingertip.

"Hey," she said. "Don't start that here. A quick skinny dip is one thing, but we'll have to go into the dunes if you want to fuck me."

Taking my finger away, I pulled the flake from my mouth and pushed it into her pussy.

"Ay-ay-ay, you fucker," she said. She panted out a few breaths and her body arced up while her pelvic region tensed. "Is that your finger still?"

"It's my flake. Every sphinx needs a tail."

"Get it out, you crazy bastard."

I pulled it out and bit one half off. "Mmmm, this is very good."

"And what about the chocolate you've melted inside me?"

"Roll onto your side and just enjoy your book," I said.

I nudged at her and she obliged, lifting her thigh to enable my head to move in. Placing my tongue just above her pubic bone, I smoothed

Cocktails

over her hair, lapped down over her clit and then sunk into her pussy. I circled around a few times to ensure I had licked off any residual chocolate and then explored the inner walls at a gentler pace.

"Oooh," she said. "How am I supposed to read with you doing that?"

I suppressed the urge to surface and gloat at superseding the book.

"Move your tongue down," she said.

She began to rock her hips and push against my mouth.

Her finger slid down past my chin and began stroking her clit. I clenched her arse cheeks in both hands and lightly brushed my fingertips in between. Her hips began gyrating harder and her breathing quickened.

"Oh, yes, keep going," she said. "Mmm, ooh, yes. I am... so... fucking... close... babe. Uh, uh, uh... oooh... nnnnnnng!"

Her pussy buzzed around my tongue and my hearing switched on and off as her thighs clamped rhythmically around my head. I broke free and let my eyes and ears readjust to the deep blue above and the occasional seagull echoing her orgasm.

"That was very nice," she said.

Before I could lift my head up, my shorts slid down over my legs and a handful of something cool slid over my cock; I caught the distinct smell of sun cream.

With her left hand squeezing my balls, her right hand made a tight fist around the base of the shaft and she began jerking me off. She was sliding her hand so fast that I had to grip her arse with my hands and press my face into her pubic hair to bear the intensity and not come too soon.

"That was really nice, but don't think I've forgotten how we got into this mess with you pushing chocolate into my cunt. So, this is your punishment."

I smothered her pubic mound with kisses and then rolled my face clear. "If this is your punishment then I am totally guilty, but I haven't learnt my lesson yet and need more punishing."

She let go with both hands. "There."

I looked down. My cock was covered in sun cream and we were not finished.

"I don't get it," I said.

Cocktails

"Having already put chocolate inside me, I am certainly not letting your cock smeared with sun cream get into me too."

"We had a date in the dunes."

"You'd best get cleaned up quick then."

I reached for my towel, but she grabbed my wrist. "Oh no you don't. That much sun cream will ruin the towel. It stains really badly."

"So… what?"

"The sea's thatta way," she said, wagging a finger back towards the waves.

"You're joking."

She picked up the camera and switched it on. "The dunes are waiting. Off you hop."

Jumping up, I ran down between our previous tracks. I could hear the shutter on the camera behind me clicking like a machine gun.

Without the motivation of following her in, the water felt much colder and I yelped as it splashed around my knees. When the first wave hit between my legs, my mouth gasped open with the shock.

I could hear her laughing in between the noise of the waves.

Needing to get the job done as quickly as possible, I splashed water up over my cock and rubbed it clear of sun cream.

Satisfied that I was sun cream free, I scrambled back up the beach.

Now entirely acclimatized to her nudity, she was up on her knees to capture my return up the beach on camera.

I jumped onto my towel and shivered.

She clambered on top of me. Her hand soon warmed up my wet cock and it recovered its hardness.

She rose up, I felt her pussy push down on my tip and then she slid her wet warmth over me. Lying down on top of me, she breathed heavily and began to thrust her hips onto me.

"I thought we were supposed to be in the dunes," I said.

"This is not the two of us," she said. "This is a new mythical creature. It has eight limbs, two heads and it is half man and half woman."

"This creature, I love."

Cocktails

Josh Redman *is a marketing copywriter currently living in Southern England. He is a keen photographer and painter and so mostly writes from visual starting points. He is particularly fascinated by the realm of dreams and the subconscious and is greatly influenced by the works of Milan Kundera and Italo Calvino. Josh has previously been published in the Stringybark anthology,* Valentine's Day.

No Regrets
— Sorcha Ni Mhaolmhuaidh

Skye approached the tattoo shop with a mixture of trepidation and excitement. She steeled herself as she heard the angry music pounding from inside the shop. Taking a deep breath, she stepped inside. It took her eyes a moment to adjust to the darkness and when they did they were drawn to the young man behind the desk. She was surprised to see that the shop was empty aside from him.

She silently berated herself for being so prejudiced. She had expected bearded, leather-clad men with the word 'Mum' inked on every extremity. This fresh-faced, good-looking man had caught her off guard.

"I have an appointment at three," she said, her voice quivering.

He looked up from his computer screen. His eyes were piercingly blue and she found it difficult to meet his gaze.

"Skye? I'm George. Just take a seat and I'll be right with you."

She watched as he prepared everything that he would need. Eventually he pulled an extra chair up beside his computer and gestured for her to sit next to him.

"So, what exactly did you have in mind?"

She took a deep breath and explained her design idea. She had given it some thought and had decided on a phrase in Italian with a watercolour effect to add some aesthetic value to an otherwise potentially clichéd tattoo. He listened intently and sketched as she talked. After about an hour they had decided on design and colour scheme. He applied a stencil to her hip and, when she was happy with positioning, he directed her to the table. She lay down and lifted her dress to display the stencil. She noticed as George's eyes flitted briefly to the black lace of her underwear.

"Ready? I'm going to start now."

She nodded, gasping as the needles pierced through her porcelain skin. Even as the pain seared she noticed how attractive he was. He had auburn hair and five o'clock shadow. His eyes were magnetic and, as he worked, his brow crinkled in concentration. She watched as his

Cocktails

skilled hands worked the ink deftly and expertly into her skin. From the corner of her eye she could see him sneaking furtive looks her way as she bit her lip to deal with the pain. His fingers traced the words developing on her hip and she couldn't help but imagine how his fingers would feel between her legs.

"Are you okay?"

His words shook her from her reverie and she blushed — worried that her eyes had betrayed her unsavoury thoughts.

"You've gone quiet. Is it hurting you?"

She shook her head fervently.

"I'm okay," she replied.

He nodded and continued to work, stopping every now and again to wipe the site clean and re-evaluate.

"Well, that's the outline done. We'll take a break before we start adding colour. Would you like a drink?" he asked.

She nodded her assent and George returned with two beers. She watched as he leaned against the wall, sipping his drink. He was wearing jeans and a baggy t-shirt but she could make out the defined body underneath.

She caught his eye and blushed again before looking away.

"Well," he said, "let's get back into it or we'll be here all night."

She took her beer back to the table and lay down again, lifting her dress to expose the developing tattoo.

They chatted as the time passed. The conversation flowed easily and she was more attracted to him as time passed. The pain of the tattoo machine seemed to only further ignite her lust and there was no denying the electricity between them. Her body tingled under his touch. She couldn't help but hope that her desire was reciprocated. Before long the whirring of the tattoo machine came to a stop.

"Well," George said, "that's us pretty much done. Stand up and let me see how it looks."

He leaned closer, examining his work. She could feel his breath on her bare skin. He ran his fingers gently over her newly-tattooed hip. He was so close to her that she felt he must be able to sense her desire. Her body trembled. George looked up and caught her eye. This time she did not look away.

Cocktails

He stood up and held her gaze wordlessly. Moving closer he kissed her lips softly, tentatively, as if waiting for her permission to continue. When she hungrily returned the gesture he kissed her roughly and lifted her dress over her head. She stood naked aside from a lace G-string. George continued to kiss her, his hands exploring her body as he did so. She pulled his shirt over his head, revealing a sculpted physique.

He picked her up and lay her down on the table. He kissed his way down her body, more gently now. She moaned as he cupped her breasts and rolled her nipples between his fingers. His eyes widened with desire as they hardened in response.

"God you're sexy," George groaned.

Skye glanced towards the shop door, knowing that anyone could walk in at any moment. The thought thrilled her.

She could feel his fingers trace the outline of her G-string. Her back arched as her body fought not to lose control.

"You're so crazily wet," he whispered.

He crept up to steal a kiss before following his fingers. She gasped with delight as she felt the wetness of his tongue between her legs. His fingers slipped inside her.

"Oh my God," she sighed.

After a few minutes George stood up and grabbed her hair. He forced her mouth close to his. As she tried to kiss him he pulled away, teasingly.

"Tell me what you want," he ordered.

She tried to kiss him again but he pulled back.

"Say it."

Her eyes traced the outline of his body.

"I want you to fuck me," she whispered.

"Say it again."

"Fuck me," she repeated, pleadingly.

He turned her so that she was facing away from him. Still holding her hair he unzipped his jeans. She could feel his erection as he pressed against her. He was so hard it hurt. She knew how good he would feel inside her but he continued to resist. The temptation was torturing her. George kissed her neck and her back, holding her tightly. His fingers slipped briefly below her waist but pulled away again – teasing her with every movement.

Cocktails

Just when Skye thought she couldn't hold on any longer he leaned her body forward and slipped inside her. She gasped with pleasure. She could feel his breath on her neck. He placed his hand across her mouth, quietening her. Her pleasure quickly built to an insurmountable level. All her pent-up desire from the afternoon had reached a climax. Her legs buckled as her orgasm rocked her body and he caught her in his strong arms. George pulled out and turned her to face him.

"Get on your knees," he growled.

She did as she was told. She traced the outline of his cock with her tongue. Her hands cupped his balls as she ran her tongue up and down his shaft. She could tell that he was aching for her to take him in her mouth but she wasn't ready for that just yet. She relished being back in control for a moment and wanted it to last. Skye stimulated him with her hands as she sucked his balls, taking one in her mouth at a time and sucking gently.

She traced the outline of her lips with the head of his cock. He sighed deeply. Eventually she relented and pulled him into her mouth. His moans thrilled her as she worked her mouth up and down his cock. She continued to caress his balls as her tongue ran the length of his shaft. She ran her tongue in circles around the head of his cock. His groans of pleasure made her so wet and she couldn't wait to have him inside her again.

She pulled back and sat on the table, spreading her legs. He grabbed her greedily and pulled himself to her again. Skye wrapped her legs around his waist — pulling him closer. Waves of pleasure washed over her.

"I'm going to come," George whispered.

She could feel the power of his body as he moved. He gripped her tighter and the feeling of being so completely in his control intensified her desire. She felt his body convulse as he came and the sensation of his body in hers triggered her own orgasm. They came simultaneously, clutching each other.

They collapsed onto the table, wrapped in each other's arms as they caught their breath. She could feel the sweat of his body as he pressed against her, panting.

Eventually George stepped back. He smiled at her and planted a gentle kiss on her forehead.

Cocktails

"Let's have a look at that tattoo, hey?"

He took her hand and led her to the mirror. Standing behind her he wiped the site and appraised the finished product. Skye smiled.

"It's perfect," she said. "Exactly what I wanted."

"Everything you thought it would be?" George asked with a wink.

"And more."

"What does it mean anyway?"

"*Senza rimpianti*? It means 'No Regrets'."

"No regrets," George repeated. "I like that."

Sorcha Ni Mhaolmhuaidh is an Irish-born/Gold Coast-based writer who tries to divide her time as evenly as possible between reading, yoga, and writing. She loves Christmas in Dublin, watercolour tattoos and Tom Robbins novels. Sorcha writes short stories and poetry and tries to bring a touch of whimsy into the life of the reader wherever possible.

Dark and Stormy
— Danielle Chedid

Eighty-nine seconds. That's how long I've been standing here. The rope bites into my palm as a particularly nasty wave rocks the ship, but it's not the sea making my stomach heave. I raise my fist to the dark wood, ready to knock, but I can't quite do it. One hundred and forty-four seconds. I take a deep breath and, before I lose my nerve, pound on the hard wood six times. And nothing. Perhaps he didn't hear me, or maybe he is asleep. I work myself up to knock again just as the door swings open.

"What is it?" His voice is grainy and his hair tousled, as if he just woke up. From bed. Where he was sleeping. *Oh dear God.*

My eyes are definitely not following the instructions my head is sending as they decide on a quick roam down the gorgeous and very naked torso of Captain Nick Davis. His chest and shoulders are well muscled and I could imagine him easily lifting me up, placing me on a ledge and ... I would trace that puckered scar that runs from his neck, dangerously close to his left nipple and tapers off —

"James!" he barks at me. I flinch, my thoughts returning to the matter at hand. Ah. That's right. I'm nervous.

"Ship! Ah, there's a ship, sir, umm, Captain." And the heat that had previously been pooling in a lower location makes a quick return to my cheeks.

"Finally!" he says, relief evident in his smile and the hearty slap my poor shoulder endures. "And whose flag catches the wind, lad?"

"The red and gold, Captain. Axe reckons we'll hit the Spanish bastards in about an hour." I reply, trying not to grin like an idiot. The word sounds less jarring than it had a few weeks ago. "Bastards." I mutter under my breath, relishing the forbidden taste of it in my mouth.

"Well get to it then lad, we need every hand on board to make this thing work."

"Aye, Captain." I tap my chest with my right fist and lower my eyes, trying to ignore the sinking feeling that returns with his words.

"James," he says. Cautiously I look back up, meeting his intense gaze. His next words are quiet, but I can't miss the compassion behind

Cocktails

them. "Take a few minutes. The first one's the worst, but they do get easier."

I feel a hot prickling behind my eyes at the kindness. "Thank..." and the door slams in my face.

I stand there, counting the seconds again as I breathe in the tangy air, itching at the binding that constricts my chest. Not for the first time, I wonder about our Captain's accent. He is clearly well educated and I can't help but wonder what drew him into the piracy business to begin with. Well, apart from his obvious love of the ocean. But he could have been out here in a way that didn't break quite so many laws. Perhaps in another life he would have been the captain of the ship we are about to commandeer.

An icy shudder passes through me and, suddenly it all feels like too much. The lies and secrecy, the filth, the piracy, the disguise; each add to the crushing weight that envelopes me. Then I see my father's condescending smirk and hear the words that sliced through my heart. *A woman is not fit to command a vessel.* I swallow the lump in my throat, and feel my resolve harden. I will be a sailor. I will be a captain. I. Will. Succeed.

No, I take it all back. This was a bad decision. A wretched decision. Probably the worst plan I have ever come up with. My breathing is shallow and I just know that I'm going to be sick. Want to know how Axe got his name? It's that wicked looking blade he carries with him everywhere — the weapon that is currently aimed at the neck of the Spanish captain. Oh dear, sweet Lord, I am going to hell.

"I'll ask ye one more time!" Axe says, raising his blade. "Where's the gold?"

"I swear," the terrified man says in a thick accent, "there is nothing!"

Axe roars and takes a wide swing.

"Enough."

The Captain's voice holds his first mate and the axe stops inches from severing the man's head from his body.

"Oh thank you! Thank you!" He collapses into a pitiful heap, sobbing with gratitude.

"Quiet!" Our captain's voice is full of command, waiting for silence.

Cocktails

"Where is the gold?"

"I – I told you, we have none!"

The Captain gives a sharp nod. One of the men flattens him to the ground while another steps on his outstretched arm.

"I don't *want* to hurt you; I'm not a barbarian." He says in that same quiet voice. "But you will not lie to me."

Suddenly Axe is there once more. The Spaniard screams. Blood coats the deck around him. The severed hand lands by my boot. I am falling.

I'm warm, snug, and covered in something wonderfully soft. It was all a terrible dream; I didn't watch an innocent man brutally lose a hand at the orders of my captain. A man who was sometimes kind and understanding, and sometimes ruthless and cruel.

As I open my eyes, reality makes a cruel return in the form of Captain Nick dozing in the bolted down swivel chair beside me.

"Oh my God." I whisper, backing as far away from him as possible. But I misjudge the length of the bed and fall to the floor in front of him. A sharp pain stabs through my left side. I try to stifle the scream that rips through my throat, but I don't quite make it in time. In an instant he is standing with sword in hand, scanning for danger.

"Don't be a fool, girl." He says, his eyes softening as he sheathes his weapon. He picks me up and places me back on his bed with the covers pulled high. "You need to rest."

"How did it happen?" I wince.

"You fell and rolled too close to one of the captives."

"Oh," I reply.

"It wasn't deep, just a flesh wound," he says as I pull my hand from my side, revealing a patch of blood seeping from my bandaged torso. My *naked* bandaged torso. And then his words hit me.

"Don't worry," he says, seeing my horrified expression, "no one else knows."

"But how did you?"

He chuckles, "I wouldn't be much of a captain if I couldn't work these things out."

"And... You don't care?" I ask, shock making me blunt.

He leans back in his chair and studies me. I'm very conscious of the fact that he has seen my naked body.

"As far as I'm concerned, you're a hard worker and adept at what you do, so why should I care what's between your legs?"

"But I don't think you're cut out for this," he says after a long moment. "Don't get me wrong, I think you *could* do it, but this sort of life wears a man down. It's a dangerous, cut-throat business, and you need to do what you have to do. Sometimes, that includes hurting other people."

"Did you — " the words catch in my throat.

"No, we didn't kill anyone," he says, looking me in the eye. "I meant it when I said I'm not a barbarian. We're here for the gold, not for the violence, so why waste a life?"

"But you cut his hand off," I whisper.

"That's one of those things that need doing." His jaw is firm and, while I can see he doesn't regret it, he doesn't gain pleasure from cruelty.

"You're not like the others," I say, looking down at our hands.

He leans forward, cupping my face with his hand and forcing me to meet his intense gaze. "Neither are you."

My breath catches and my skin tingles where his hand touches me. And suddenly, I don't want to be alone. I want to feel his skin on mine, in every place possible. I want to touch, kiss, hold, caress. I want to feel alive.

"Come here," I say, my voice throaty with lust.

"That's probably not a good idea." He looks uneasy.

So I move to him, straddling him in the chair as I press my lips to his. His hands grasp my hips as I loosen the ties at his shirt. My fingers trail lower, tugging open the buttons of his trousers, until I feel his hard cock pressed against my palm. He groans as I grasp him and move up and down, lightly at first, but faster as I feel him responding.

"Stop," he grunts, pulling away. "You're injured."

And with that he stands and lowers me on to the bed. But before he can move any further, I grab him with both hands and take him in my mouth.

"Oh God," he moans as I increase the pressure.

I alternate between hard and fast, and soft licks on the sensitive head.

Cocktails

I pull his pants down the rest of the way before I release him and tug him down to me. In seconds, his mouth is all over my body, kissing my face, my neck and trailing down to my bare breast. I gasp as his tongue passes over my nipple and my legs open of their own accord. He pulls my loose pants off before stepping between them, lowering himself until he pushes against my wetness.

"Are you sure?" His eyes are dark and stormy with need and I can feel the self-control he's using just to ask the question.

"Yes." And he thrusts into me. "Yes!" I scream. "Oh God, yes!"

I have been with men before, but none have made me feel this. With each thrust, warmth shoots up through my body, the pleasure growing, building, becoming more intense. I'm hardly aware of what he's doing now, except for the need for him to keep going; harder, faster, deeper. And then I'm there. The heat, the pressure, this intense *feeling* can no longer be contained. My whole body arches as I scream, digging my nails into his tense buttocks as he rocks me into oblivion. But it doesn't stop. He keeps up the pace and in no time, another powerful wave blasts through my body. This time I'm aware of him pulling out and groaning with his own release. Then he lies back down and I burrow into the crook of his arm, deep in thought.

"What happens now?" I ask, looking up into those deep blue pools.

"That's up to you."

Danielle Chedid *lives in Perth and has just finished her undergraduate degree in psychology. She plans on becoming a teacher, inflicting her love of reading and writing on her students. When she can find a spare minute in between studying and working, she loves spending time with her wonderful boyfriend and family.*

Deep Dark Secret
— Claire Martijn

He sat at the table, in the room designated as his home office. Home office. Funny choice of words. Really it was the junk room with a space he had managed to clear in order for his laptop and other work paraphernalia to be placed; a room he could escape the noisy clutter of household chaos. It was a late Friday evening. He was alone. His wife was… somewhere. She had told him, kind of, as she had left, shouting up the stairs in his general direction before slamming the door. Something about visiting a work colleague. He hadn't even deigned to reply; after all she wouldn't have stopped to listen anyway. That courtesy had ceased quite some time ago.

The laptop clicked and hummed as it turned on. Tonight he had to clean it out. His new laptop had arrived the day before and the youngest of his brother's children had reminded him that this now antiquated laptop had been promised to them. Hence the need to clean it. Goodness knows what could found on it. Apart from sensitive work documents, there were pass codes to personal accounts, banking and all manner of other documents and pictures… He paused. It had been almost a year now, since he had last looked at his private Dropbox file. There in the recesses of that application, buried far away, was a folder he had dared not delve into for eight long agonising months. His deep dark secret. Did he dare to now?

He sat back and stared at the computer screen. The background was a beautiful picture of majestic towering trees with a path winding secretly between them, up and out onto a sun covered mountainside. She had never been there, but had commented on the picture he had sent her, the previous year, and since then he had kept it openly on display, an innocent picture with a secret meaning. He wouldn't change that screen saver just as he wouldn't delete the file. No matter what anyone would ever say to him, the file containing so many memories collected in a relatively short space of time, were held just as dear to him as the memories of his own family — perhaps more so. He just didn't know if he should open the file and look at them now or just quickly and safely transfer the contents to a newer secure location.

Cocktails

So he sat and pondered. He was alone, he reasoned. It had been almost a year, so what harm could there be?

With a few clicks and tapping passwords and code keys the file opened and unfolded its contents. They spilled forth in a blaze that triggered synapses and reignited memories he had held tenuously at bay. Picture upon picture, thousands of them. Sunsets, sunrises, a kaleidoscope of things. Pictures he had sent her and she had sent him, pictures they had taken together. There were written documents, emails, recordings, songs, such a multitude of collected items that he blinked, surprised by the sheer volume. How could he have forgotten that there was so much? So much emotion buried beneath the everyday mundane in the hopes of doing the right thing. The right thing... quickly he shouldered the thought aside. It irked him no end. Day and night he pushed and swept that under the carpet and now was not the time to face that truth. He shook his head and leant in towards the screen.

He flicked through a few of the emails, smiled at some of the silly things that had been sent and received as attachments. Some trivial some ridiculous, some serious and newsworthy, but the typed words in each email cut him. Tiny Xs and smiley faces. Hearts and miss yous.

He glanced at the long list of songs. Refused to play any. Already he felt a tightness in his chest.

There was a file filled with poems. He dared not venture in there for fear of losing his composure and then he came across a single item, a video clip.

He caught his breath.

Without realising it he had activated the play button and there she stood.

There was no noise, the quality was a little fuzzy, it was quite obviously a home video. But she was glorious. She moved slowly. The morning light soft, coming from one angle. It highlighted the tilt of her breast under the clinging top as she turned slightly. Her hands skimmed down her sides before grasping its hem and lifted the offending material up and over her head.

He gasped. *Oh my. She is so beautiful.*

Her hands grazed her breasts before cupping one, fingers pulling at the large nipple. Oh, how he had loved to suck those nipples. Tease one,

Cocktails

then the other, taunt and pull, pinch and illicit soft moans from her. Her nipples would harden as he would roll them between his fingers, sucking and gently biting and them making her shudder. Her head tilted back, exposing her long neck and her other hand slipped south, smoothly over her hip angling inwards to halt with her fingers splayed below her softly rounded belly and above the dark neatly trimmed thatch that barely hid her sex.

He moaned and shifted in his seat. Memories of them together crowded his mind.

On screen she continued to fondle her breast. That itself was a sight to see, she was obviously enjoying the sensation. He squirmed and readjusted himself, feeling suddenly restricted in his jeans. It was her other hand that now captivated his attention. It had shifted, lowered itself and was deftly caressing the folds he had once caressed. Her legs spread and he inched forward, face closer to the screen, trying in vain to see more of what he now vividly remembered. His love of pleasing her, seeing her desire for him had always been his undoing. He licked his lips as her fingers disappeared only to re-emerge glistening and wet. With every undulation of her hips he squirmed until without another thought he unzipped and in a sigh of relief, allowed his cock to spring forth. He watched as her fingers flicked and rubbed her clitoris, his own hand around himself, pumping in slow unison. She twisted her nipple and delved deeper, slid her nimble fingers along her cleft and worked herself and him into a heightened sense of urgent need. He was there, back in her house. Her slender arms wrapped around his chest as she kissed his jaw, pulled with her teeth his lower lip. Her legs sliding along his, their torsos covered in a fine layer of sweat as they roused sensations erotic and raw. Her words and declarations of love that he hung upon, that engulfed him and lent more urgency to his own love for her. He had never felt more alive, more needed and more loved. Suddenly he gasped, knowing he couldn't halt the sensation building inside, not wanting to and refusing to. He snatched a handful of tissues from a box nearby, pumped himself hard, shuddering in a shouting climax as he watched her toss her head, her hips jerk, breasts thrust out and up, those beautiful nipples erect and pebble hard, before she curled inwards. The video ended.

Cocktails

He panted. Stared at the frozen last scene. Her face partially captured, looking directly at the camera, eyes wide full of emotions, content in the relief of having physically orgasmed yet overflowing with loneliness and need. A promise of future love if only he was daring enough to collect it.

The sound of someone knocking on her door late at night caused her to frown. The pure fact that her dog hadn't made a sound made her curious. The sensor light was activated and she flicked on extra outdoor lighting before opening the interior door, knowing the outer security screen was locked.

Her dog was sitting patiently at his feet, tongue lolling from between its gaping jaws, doggie smile as though saying, "Look who's home, Mum!"

She stood, quiet, just looking, drinking in the sight before her. Locked her knees to keep her legs from shaking and willed herself to keep breathing. She refused to be the first to say anything. He had come to her.

"Am I too late?" His voice rolled through her senses, warm liquid gold, heating her inner core curling low and settling in to smoulder, causing an achy need to surface.

She tilted her head. She clearly remembered the occasion when she had surmised a similar situation long ago, when, if he had decided to return to his wife that within a year he would be back or at the very least contacting her, knowing the choice he had made was not to last.

"That depends." She replied softly.

Her voice sounded like heaven. He almost cried. He wanted desperately to touch her. *Damn this locked screen.*

She tried not to stare at his mouth. She could see his nervousness — his concentration plainly evident by his lip chewing. Her fingers twitched, she wanted to touch his lips. To feel their softness to have his mouth... she blinked rapidly, swallowed and forced her mind to focus on his words.

"Depends on what?" he managed to say, sounding calm and in control, surprising himself.

"On how long you intend to stay?"

Cocktails

He gazed at her. She stood before him, bathed from behind in soft candlelight. She wore little; it was summer and the night balmy. A short skirted dress of some light gauzy material, bra-less, hinting at her breasts and dusky nipples. She looked divine. The outdoor light threw shadows over her face. She neither smiled nor frowned. Composed. He wondered how she could stand there, not knowing that he was to have been arriving, knocking on her door so suddenly out of the blue? She seemed so damned controlled, when he himself was a bundle of mixed nerves. Would she turn him away? Was he too late?

"Forever." He spoke softly yet firmly.

She nodded in a manner as though saying, "Oh… okay… really… and I should believe you because?"

He gestured to the neighbouring house. "It's for sale. I'll be your neighbour."

She half smiled, leant forward and unlocked the latch, pushing the screen partially open. "Well," she breathed "don't waste your money on that place." He stepped inside and she added in a half whisper, as though fearing the reply. "Can I ask why now?"

He touched her cheek and she unconsciously leaned into his palm. "A lot of things…"

"But…?" she prompted. "The catalyst?"

He gazed at her intently and saw that same wide-eyed emotional plea. "The video," he replied and knew he was finally home.

Claire Martijn has always had a passion for writing. She attributes much of her inspiration these days to her handsome partner, J, whether that be stories of varied genre, poetry or in-depth outpourings of emotive thought-provoking writings or 'drivel' as she terms it. Written words vie for space in her everyday. Claire currently lives on the NSW south coast with her son and their dog.

Screaming Orgasm
— Maria Bonar

1971, a hot January night in Punt Road, Prahran. Me and Kev had left the Max Hotel earlier. Kev wanted to have a naughty before his flat mate, Wayne, had the chance to stagger home and interrupt us, like he did the weekend before when I stayed over.

Me and Kev were still a bit shy with each other. I wasn't a virgin when we met, but he was. I didn't have that much experience, just the usual back seat groping and fumbling in an 'S' Series Valiant at the drive in. To be honest, my first boyfriend never even took my knickers off, just pulled them to one side and in he went. Thirty seconds and it was all over.

I was really keen on Kev. I didn't want him to think I was a bit of a moll because I done it before, so I just lay back quietly and let him go for it, acting as if I wasn't that interested. It was maddening, to tell the truth. All that fingering and stroking beforehand got me all stirred up, but as usual, it ended when Kev did. Too soon.

Kev had rolled off me and was almost asleep, while I throbbed with heat and frustration. I lay there listening to the cicadas, when suddenly the door was thrown open and light filled the room as Wayne staggered in with a dark haired older woman.

"Hey," he smiled, "Sorry to wake youse up. This is Vonny."

"Jeez mate, put the light out," said Kev, blinking. He leant over and switched on the dim bedside lamp as Wayne snapped the overhead light off again.

I pulled the sheet up to my chin as Vonny yacked and Wayne poured everyone a beer. Wayne sat on the lounge chair facing us. Vonny wedged herself beside him, her mini skirt riding up to show a scrap of lacy knickers and a lot of tanned flesh. Wayne drank his beer, his arm around Vonny. His hand moved down to fondle her backside before wandering further, snagging the leg of her knickers open, his finger sliding into her crack. She obligingly spread her legs wider and leaned over to kiss him, open-mouthed.

I held my breath. Kev stirred beside me as he copped an eyeful of

Cocktails

Wayne's fingers stretching and leisurely sliding in and out of Vonny's bush in the dim glow of the lamp.

When Vonny started breathing faster and moaning, Wayne put his beer down, freeing his other hand. He unbuttoned her blouse, fondling and squeezing her tits. His lips soon followed.

Kev pulled me closer, spooning me, his breath hot in my ear. Copying Wayne, he pushed my legs apart and slid his finger into my crack. Still watching, he followed Wayne's finger symphony, note for note, playing me like a guitar; a five finger exercise plucking and twanging. I trembled as a deep tingling radiated from my belly to my groin. Kev's cock nudged between my thighs. Like Vonny, I spread my legs for more.

Kev switched the lamp off and pulled the sheet over our heads. He moved his fingers out of my crack to my clit, pinching it as he slid the warm, rounded head of his cock tightly into me from behind. This time as Kev pushed deeper and harder, bedsprings creaking in time, the quivering and tingling built up to a breathtaking crescendo, convulsive waves of pleasure crashing over me.

When my breathing returned to normal, I heard Wayne and Vonny stumble towards his bed, the headboard bumping against the wall as he tripped over his dacks. They fell together onto the mattress, the moonlight from the window shading their bodies in black and silver.

Unlike our sneaky roll in the hay, Wayne and Vonny gave it everything, pawing at each other on top of the bed as we sneaked a look at them.

Vonny sang out, "No, no, no, no," between gulping breaths, as she wrapped her legs around him, frantically thrusting herself forward. Wayne grunted and panted over her like a caveman.

When her tune changed from "no, no, no, no," to "harder, harder, harder," rising to a screaming orgasm, me and Kev burst into a wild fit of giggles.

"Ignorant bastards!" Vonny yelled. "We never laughed when youse were playing up."

This made us snort even louder as we tried to smother our laughs under the covers. Eventually, everything went quiet.

When I woke next morning, I was glad to see that Wayne's bed was

Cocktails

empty. I was pleasantly sore between my legs and the sheets smelled of sweat and cum. I stroked Kev's cock, remembering how good it felt last night. Kev lay back as I gave him French kisses, slow and deep. When he was rock hard he tried to roll me over, but I pushed him down and threw my leg over him. I rubbed myself against him, covering his belly with snail trails. When I was ready I opened up to take the length of him, as deep as it would go.

"I'm gonna root you, this time," I told him. I slid up and down, rubbing my clit hard against him, slowly at first, then faster and faster until I came in a glorious explosion of noise and juices.

That's how it was after that. I wasn't shy any more about pleasing myself when I was feeling randy. I never met Vonny again after her one-night-stand with Wayne, but I was always grateful to her for giving me the green light in ditching my hang-ups. A lifetime of noisy pleasure lay ahead of me.

*Scots born, **Maria Bonar** lives in Perth, Western Australia. Now retired from management and research roles in the corrections and health fields, she writes short fiction, articles and the occasional poem. She is currently the vice president and newsletter editor of the* Society of Women Writers WA.

Make Believe
— Robin Storey

The door opened to reveal a tall, thin man in a three-piece evening suit, his face hidden behind a devil's mask, complete with two stiff horns.

"Good evening. You must be Peter and Jocelyn." He gave an exaggerated sweep of his arm. "Entrez."

On a sideboard in the entrance hall was a large crate, full of masks.

"Choose a mask," the devil ordered. Pete chose a Batman mask and Joss decided on a rosy-cheeked young face with golden plaits attached to it, which she assumed was Goldilocks. Sweet and innocent, very apt. Well, innocent, anyway. Although she considered herself broadminded, she'd never been to one of these nights. She took a deep breath to steady her racing heart.

"I've had these masks especially made," the devil said as they were putting them on. "They're made from a lightweight latex that allows your skin to breathe so you don't get too hot. You've also a decent-sized hole for your mouth so you can eat and drink — and any other oral activities you fancy."

They followed him into a large, plush living room, buzzing with groups of masked guests in formal evening wear as required by the dress code. A bar ran along one wall, tended by two bartenders wearing zombie masks. Vampire waiters glided around offering canapés.

"No real names, please," the devil said. "Use your character's name or make one up."

He motioned to one of the bartenders. "Two more *Make Believes*, please." He took them both by the elbow. "Now's the time to separate. Don't be shy — you're not the only first-time swingers here tonight."

He propelled Joss over to the nearest group, consisting of The Joker from Batman, King Kong, Minnie Mouse and Cleopatra. "Folks, this is Goldilocks. This is her first time tonight, so be gentle with her." He steered Pete over to the other side of the room.

"It's my first time tonight too," The Joker said. His muscular physique was evident even under his evening suit.

Cocktails

A waiter appeared beside Joss. "Your *Make Believe* cocktail, Madam." It was frothy pink, garnished with a mint leaf. Joss took several slurps through the straw. It was deliciously potent. A couple of these and all her inhibitions would evaporate.

"Whoa there, Goldilocks," King Kong said. "You'll pass out in your porridge if you're not careful."

He oozed sleaziness, even through his mask. Minnie Mouse gave a polite laugh and Cleopatra looked away. *I'm definitely not fucking King Kong.*

As the group bantered and joked, Joss watched The Joker. Something about him was disturbingly familiar.

"What made you decide to come?" she asked him.

"It was Carole's idea — whoops, sorry, no names. She thought it would revive our marriage. Frankly, I think it's past resuscitation."

Holy shit. Carole. It was now horribly clear. The man standing in front of her was Andrew Marks. Her boss. Or one of them. There were three partners in the law firm, and he was the one most disliked by the staff — when he wasn't ignoring them, he was bawling them out for some slight misdemeanour. There'd been rumours that his marriage was on the rocks and that was why he was so cantankerous. And he was disguised as The Joker. It would be hilarious if it wasn't so appalling. *I'm not fucking him, either.*

"And what about you?" he said.

She could feel his gaze upon her, burning through his mask, and a reciprocal heat warmed her insides and moved down her body.

"My boyfriend wanted to give it a go," she said, in a high-pitched tone so he wouldn't recognise her voice. Not that it was likely, as he hardly took any notice of her in the office.

"Interesting," he replied. "We're both virgin swingers and we're here to please our partners. We've got something in common."

Joss nodded and took another slurp of her drink. His raw masculine energy was almost palpable. Her nipples hardened against the soft silk of her evening gown. How come she'd never noticed before how sexy he was? Maybe it was the cocktail. *There's no way I'm fucking my boss. Mask or not.*

A bell tinkled and the devil took the floor. "Ladies and gentlemen,

Cocktails

I'd like to welcome you to our Masked Strangers Night. There are only two rules. The first is not to force yourself on anyone — if they say no, you must respect that. And secondly, in the spirit of the theme, please leave your masks on and don't divulge your identity. You can try out a new persona or act out your wildest fantasy in the knowledge that no-one will know who you are. When you're ready for action, there are plenty of rooms on this floor and the one below. And rule number three — have fun!"

A few couples dispersed. Others hung around the bar. Batman disappeared with a curvy Marg Simpson. Joss barely had time to stifle a pang of jealousy before a strong arm encircled her waist. A voice breathed in her ear, "I'm not sure of the etiquette here — do I ask you if you'd like to fuck?"

Without waiting for a reply, The Joker kissed her softly all around her earlobe. The warmth inside her had reached her pussy, which was positively tingling. He took her hand and led her out of the living room and down the hall.

Say you've got a headache. Or rabies. Anything! As her mind considered a range of afflictions, her legs followed him down the hallway. All the rooms were occupied, except for a room at the end, a small study containing a desk and a leather chair.

"This'll do," The Joker said. He pulled her inside and closed the door. He slid the top of her evening dress down, exposing her breasts, and nibbled each nipple. The only affliction she had now was a clit that felt as if it would explode if it didn't get some attention soon.

He straightened up. "This mask is annoying me. What say we take them off? No-one will know."

"No!" Joss said quickly. "I mean, it'll spoil the fun. Let's keep them on."

The Joker shrugged. "Okay. As long as you don't want to do any role play, I'm no good at that. Now, where were we?"

He continued sliding her dress down, trailing kisses down her belly. As her skin quivered under his lips, the words "Role Play" flashed in neon lights in her mind, followed instantly by "Revenge." Just as he was about to expose her knickers, she gripped his shoulders.

"Stop! Go into the corner and face the wall!"

He paused. "What's going on?"
"Just do as I say! You'll find out soon enough!"
He got up slowly. "Is this some sort of kinky game?"
"Did I say you could ask a question?"
That's for grunting at me when I say "Good Morning" to you.
He shrugged, walked over to the back corner and stood facing it. Joss slid off her dress and knickers and still wearing her heels, hoisted herself on to the desk.
"Now take off your clothes!"
"So it *is* a kinky game. I hope there's no whipping involved."
"Your hopes don't concern me in the least. Clothes off, now!"
That's for accusing me of misplacing the office security keys when you had them all the time. And you didn't even apologise.
She watched him as he undressed. His body was every bit as delicious as she'd imagined — as smooth and taut as a Roman statue.
Joss leaned back on the desk and parted her legs. "Now turn around."
He did as he was told. His cock was hard and pointing straight at her, even before he set eyes on her plumply gleaming pussy.
"This is my sort of game," he said. "Permission to approach, Madam."
"Permission denied," Joss snapped. "Stay right where you are."
That's for making me do that urgent job in my lunch hour and missing my lunch date.
She opened her legs wider so he got a good view and started stroking her pussy, only occasionally caressing her clit as she was almost on the brink and didn't want to come just yet. The Joker's breathing was ragged and his cock looked as if any moment it would break free from him and launch itself at her pussy.
"Now you can approach," she commanded.
"You're one hell of a sexy woman," he said as he stood before her. He reached out and she slapped his hand away. "The only tongue I want from you is on my clit. And make it snappy, I need some relief."
That's for ...what's it for? Slipped my mind....
He was crouched in front of her, his warm tongue circling her clit, teasing it until she couldn't bear it, and when his tongue finally found it, a rush of warmth flooded her, then she was moaning and bucking on

Cocktails

the desk, papers flying on to the floor. As she lay there, breathless and tingling, she felt his cock nudging her pussy. She sat up.

"Oh no, you don't."

That's for telling anti-feminist jokes at the work Christmas party.

She hauled herself off the desk and motioned to it. "On there, on your back."

"You're also one hell of a bossy woman."

"When I want your opinion, I'll ask for it. Which will be never."

That's for the time you ignored me when I wanted to make a suggestion at the staff meeting.

He clambered on to the desk and lay on his back, cock pointing to the ceiling. "Suck me, please," he begged. She longed to put her mouth around it, but he'd enjoy that too much.

"Sorry, that's not on the agenda."

That's for always forgetting my name. I don't think you ever knew it.

She climbed on to the desk, lowered herself on to his cock and slid up and down, varying her tempo and stopping when she sensed he was nearing climax. "You sexy bitch," he groaned, and then she felt his cock pulsing inside her and he was gasping and clutching her buns.

She removed his hands from her butt, climbed off him and began to dress, leaving him spreadeagled on the desk, still panting, cock limply sated.

"I'm off," she said. "Tidy up, please and clean up the wet splotch on the desk."

And as she opened the door, "And don't forget to turn off the light."

And that's for everything else.

On Monday morning, as she walked into the office, her co-worker Angie greeted her with, "Guess what! Andrew came in this morning whistling! And he smiled at me and said "Good morning!" Can you believe it?"

"Absolutely not," Joss said.

"Something drastic must have happened on the week-end. Maybe he got his rocks off."

Joss smiled. "Maybe."

Cocktails

Robin Storey *is an author and freelance writer from the Sunshine Coast in Queensland.* She has written two novels, comedy crime How Not To Commit Murder *and romantic comedy* Perfect Sex, *both available on* Amazon *and* Smashwords. *She is working on her third novel and enjoys writing short stories as a break from the marathon of novel writing. This is her first erotic short story. Robin would love to connect with you on her blog www.storey-lines.com.*

White Russian
— Julie Davies

Intimate relationships between team members were strictly against the rules. Major Maria-Angela Berlusconi understood its necessity for the gaggle of scientists and engineers confined on the Taurus-Littrow Lunar Station on two-year tours of duty. She could well imagine life might become rather fraught if you had a romantic bust-up on a moon base. It wasn't as though you could storm out and sever all contact. Then there were the opportunities for revenge. How easy would it be for a rejected lover to open an airlock after the object of their disaffection had already de-suited? She'd accepted the restriction and resigned herself to two years of abstinence.

She realised she'd probably been chosen for the role of Chief Geologist simply because she was a dutiful plodder, not known for intemperate behaviour. She couldn't afford to be. After all this time, the legend of her notorious great-grandfather's antics at the helm of Italy in the noughties, or perhaps that should be naughties, still floated in her wake like lunar dust. The speculative looks cast her way by new acquaintances embarrassed her, until one day she decided: "*Che cazzo!* I'll go my own way and to hell with them all." Perhaps Nonno Silvio hadn't been entirely diluted from her genes, after all.

Half way through her first tour, Vlad The Impaler arrived from the Triumphal Union of Russian Democracies to supervise the heat flow experiments. She soon discovered what a prime example of nominative determinism that turned out to be. Vlad managed to swagger even in one-sixth gravity and had serious researchers of both genders swooning like love-sick teenagers. He boasted that 'Vlad' meant ruler. She could only assume that referred to twelve inches of wood, after observing his silhouette as he spied on Veronique bending over the hydroponic lettuces. The reason for his nickname 'The Impaler' became apparent after their first encounter outside the showers.

Maria-Angela had endured a restless night, after making the mistake of reading *Madame Bovary* again. For nearly a year, she'd ignored the

Cocktails

sharp reminders of celibacy her body gave every time she hastily soaped herself under the mandatory two-minute shower. Some tiny, lingering dart of Catholic guilt left her reluctant to pleasure herself.

This time, while reading a steamy encounter between Emma and Rodolphe, she found herself fingering one nipple. A surge of lust ripped unbidden through her body, in a direct line from nipple to vagina. She abandoned her tablet beside the bunk and explored her already wet slit. The clitoris swelled under her finger, popping out of its protective sheath like the warning button on Nonna's antique steam cooker. She circled it softly and moved into a smooth rhythm, around and down to the pulsating cavern below. Within moments she was convulsing, bouncing several centimetres off the standard issue mattress. She kept her mouth tightly closed so her colleagues wouldn't hear her through the thin walls of the dorm. She lay spent, gasping and delighted.

"Why did it take me so long? What a blessed release. That should do me for a while."

She was wrong. Her awakened libido built up momentum like an avalanche. The last pulsation of sated lust didn't die away but gathered more energy. Within minutes she was stroking, need and greed sweeping her away. She looked desperately around the room, searching for something to fill her aching void. Keeping her right hand on the joy button, she reached over to the toilet bag on the table and grabbed a deodorant stick. She slid it between her oozing lips, walls gripping, as she thrust it deep inside her; in and out, in time with the merry-go-round above. The orgasm shook her to the core, muscles contracting so urgently the deodorant shot out across the room and hit the aluminium wall with a clang. Her long groan ended in a high-pitched squeal, echoed only minutes later all around her. She had set the whole female dorm off.

Shame confined her to the bunk until her holographic San Marco clock showed four o'clock. But the avalanche hadn't yet come to its final resting place. She could still feel a visceral stirring but she daren't touch herself again. If she were lucky, her colleagues hadn't located the source of the original moaning. But she couldn't risk losing control a second time. What she needed was a cold shower.

She slipped on her bathrobe and padded barefoot to the ablution block. As she passed the lone porthole in the western wall of the

Cocktails

corridor, she saw the first rays of the sun peek over the horizon, dazzling even this early, without any atmosphere to filter it. She reached the showers just as Vlad emerged naked, water slowly dribbling in large, discrete droplets down his smooth olive-skinned chest. She stopped dead, watching his cock instantly stand to attention. It was every bit as impressive as she'd imagined. She raised her eyes to his face, as his chiselled lips slid into a knowing grin. Dark eyebrows framed intense blue eyes, one brow lifting in question. Her powerful intellect and all discretion retreated to her genitals, as she parted her robe.

"Stand at ease, Lieutenant."

Vlad was there in a flash, impaling her as she raised one leg to encircle his hips. One paw gripped her buttock and pulled her against him, the other clawed her breast up to his mouth, as he bent his head to suck at her. His roughness hurt but the pain became enmeshed in the pleasure, frightening and thrilling. Two hard thrusts had her pressed against the back wall of the corridor. She arched her pelvis upward and his cock penetrated to her core. Her mind fixated helplessly on their groins, locked in a low-gravity dance. Each thrust bounced her further along the corridor, closer to the dorms.

She lost concentration, as she realised how easily they could be discovered. Climax evaded her. Seconds later, his stomach muscles tensed and he thrust back his head. He came silently and didn't bring her with him. Stepping back, the White Russian wiped himself on *her* bathrobe and sauntered away with a smug smile. "You come back here," she hissed to his retreating back. "You owe me!"

Maria-Angela watched Vlad the Dud Root clamber into a lunar rover and exit the complex, heading for their transport hub near Steno Crater. She was in luck. She'd seen on the roster he was meeting an Automated Transfer Vehicle from Guiana there and the grunts to unload it wouldn't be on duty for hours. She was damned-well going to do a site-inspection and claim her rightful due. After setting up the day's tasks for her staff, she commandeered the base's other rover and drove out to Steno.

The ATV had landed and Vlad had already connected it to the primary docking station when she arrived. She drove into the vehicular entrance and passed through the airlock. Peeling off her compression suit, she hurried down the corridor to the cargo bay.

Vlad looked surprised as she clomped in, clad only in regulation thermal underwear and boot liners. He did seem genuinely pleased to see her, as the tented crotch of his overalls attested.

"I don't think much of your sexy knickers, *lapushka*, but what the hell," he grinned.

"I've come for what you owe me."

"Is that an order, Major?"

"Affirmative. I want it and I want it now."

Maria-Angela brazened it out, although she had no idea how Vlad would react to a dominating woman. She needn't have worried. He approached her with an intent frown of concentration, hands expertly stripping the granddad garments from her shivering limbs. He was gentler this time, leading her to a pallet of padded cartons. She draped herself across one and Vlad knelt before her, parting her legs. She leaned back, closed her eyes, as his tongue teased her folds. He swirled the tip around and around her clit, in perfect synchrony with his two fingers thrusting inside, expertly massaging.

She was in ecstasy. If a physicist was this good, she was going to try a biologist next time. She came again and again, writhing under his touch.

The earth moved — no really. The floor of the vehicle began shaking and she opened her eyes to see Vlad standing over her, eyes wide in alarm.

"Fuck! That's the fusion drive. It's not supposed to reignite for another 36 earth hours. Quick! We better get out."

"What?"

"It's automated. ATVs stay for a programmed time while we unload them, then take off. But this one is obviously faulty. Get up! We've got to leave. NOW!"

Maria-Angela jumped to her feet. She scrambled for her underwear and hopped about, trying to pull them on.

"You don't have time," he squeaked, grabbing them from her and racing to the airlock. Urgency and fear had raised his voice an octave.

She chased after him and the internal airlock door closed behind them. Vlad surged through just as the outer door was closing but it swooshed shut in her face. She was trapped! Before long, the force of acceleration drove her to the floor and she lay immobilised, too terrified to do anything.

Cocktails

Major Doctor Maria-Angela Berlusconi stared down at the Moon, fast retreating below. Her worksite was 4.5 billion years old, only 100 million years younger than the Earth. Her job had been to look for evidence to support the theory it had been birthed in a collision between the infant Earth and another planet.

She should have stuck to the rules. They'd never let her back now. She would arrive at the Guiana Launch Centre naked and humiliated, the security footage already being forensically examined by the authorities, no doubt. Twitterverse would be alive with clips of Vlad The Tonguer and Berlusconi The Supine within 24 hours. Her career was over.

David Bowie's *Space Oddity* had become the astronaut anthem after some Canadian on the International Space Station revived it forty years ago and she knew every word. She sang under her breath: "Ground Control to Major Twat."

Earth rose from below the ATV as it accelerated in a parabolic arc, framing the Moon in a blue halo. Its beauty took her breath away. She'd been securely strapped in and unable to see anything on her inward journey. Tears filled her eyes; tears of regret for the extraordinary life she had just forfeited. But it could have been worse. If she'd been trapped in the storage area of the ATV, the oxygen would have been extracted. She'd have paid the ultimate price for her indiscretions, just like Madame Bovary. That bloody woman had started this whole mess. Damn her to hell.

Although Maria-Angela had to admit she had experienced the ride of her life, in more ways than one.

Julie Davies is a novelist and short story writer from Central Queensland. She has had ten stories published in nine Stringybark anthologies, her latest in Valentine's Day, *and twenty-five published in other anthologies, literary journals and online magazines. She'll continue writing short stories to motivate herself while she reels from the rejections of her first (non-erotic) novel and struggles with the second. This story is one of an erotic collection she is writing on the deadliest sin through the ages.*

Lychee Martini
— Dusty Lane

If I ever again venture down to Wan Chai for another lychee martini wearing my *Herve Leger* dress, I must remember not to wear knickers.

Wearing that dress had always made me feel horny. Not wearing knickers makes me feel horny too. Hot weather, Hong Kong, a few champagnes before dinner, then a few more champagnes, even hornier! My mind's screensaver had reset automatically to sex. Earlier, I had noticed the pretty girl seated near the bar with a group having dinner. Her eyes followed me as I walked past. In fact, she 'undressed' me as I walked. It wouldn't have taken her long. There wasn't much to undress. No bra, no knickers.

I pushed into the crowd at the bar to get our next bottle, as I stood in the crush pressing forward to be served, I noticed perfume. Intrigued, I turned and she was right behind me. Red lipstick. Short dark hair, heart-shaped face. Pretty, gorgeous, about my height. I could feel her knee touching the back of my thigh. Maybe it was just unavoidable in the bar crush. I opened my stance slightly, sliding my feet apart — not always easy to do in these *Louboutins*.

Moments later, there was no mistaking the touch of a hand. Two fingers, palm up, slid between my thighs. Pushing forward, gently. Until it stopped right there. Holy Smokes! I thought, without even a 'howdy-do-di'! I half turned and she stood there smiling ... looking as smug and as innocent as Sylvester having just grabbed Tweetie Pie.

She had summed me up perfectly. I didn't say anything. I didn't slap her hand. I don't know how but she knew that I was in the mood for something ridiculously outrageous. I shifted forward as an open spot at the bar appeared to my left. As expected she stayed right behind me. To order the champagne, I had to lean further forward to be heard above the music. Her next foray was just as accurate as her first. I'd only just finished saying *Veuve*, when her tall man hit the 'bull's eye'.

It's hot and steamy in August in Hong Kong. And in this crowded bar I was too. And she was throwing fuel on the fire. Her finger slid back

Cocktails

and around my pussy, just as the champagne arrived. My body was all a-tingle. I paid cash and took the bottle.

She looked at me, smiled, and as she pressed a coaster into my free hand, said, "You're hot, babe."

Still somewhat stunned, all I could muster was a smile before I crossed the few metres back to our table. I put the bottle into the ice bucket and then noticed that another new bottle had arrived while I was at the bar. I sat thinking of all the things I should've said and fumed that I didn't manage to get even a word out. I watched her make her way back to hers. She didn't get anything while at the bar. But maybe she got exactly what she wanted.

My mind was racing. I'd never been fingered in a bar before. It was … deliciously smutty, and good. I knew there was nothing else that was going to scratch this itch … an itch that was still building. The idea of later going back to my hotel alone after that encounter had zero appeal. Not tonight. Certainly not while wearing this dress. I put the coaster in my clutch as I checked my phone.

As soon as both new bottles were finished, I made my farewells and walked to the lift lobby. I called the number on the coaster while waiting for the lift. Her husky voice answered.

"Hello. Who's this?" she asked.

"Did you just give me your number at the bar?"

"Oh, it's you." She paused. "I can't see you but … um, hi."

"Hi, I'm Karen."

"Hi. Where are you?"

As the lift door opened, I said, "I'm downstairs. I … I hope you're still hungry. Dessert is ready. But you'll have to hurry."

She was there in minutes. Once we were outside on the pavement, she hailed a cab and gave him directions in Cantonese. As the crappy old honkers taxi inched into the traffic, she slid closer to me and asked, "Would you like to come back to my place?"

"I'm staying at the Langham Place."

"Okay, we can go there. Just as easy," she replied and then in Cantonese she instructed the driver to take the tunnel to Mongkok.

A few awkward moments passed as I frantically tried to think of

Cocktails

something, anything to say. I asked if her name was pronounced Li or Ly. "Just like the fruit," she replied. It was a response that she'd, no doubt, used once or twice before. Her fingers moved down my arm. Once her hand reached my thigh, we were back on course. My lack of underwear once again prevented any realistic restriction on Miss Lychee and I happily let her do all the work.

She kissed me quickly while the driver was preoccupied with the toll. By the time we pulled into the hotel driveway, I'd straightened my dress and was pleased that my knickers were in my hotel room and not on the floor of the taxi. We went straight to the private lift and up to the 32nd floor. I smiled at the cameras in the lift before I kissed her. This time she let me take the lead. I pressed against her and pushed my hand under her dress. Suspenders! Nice touch, I thought, as I felt the softness of her skin. My hand took hold of her butt and pulled her to me. She kissed my ear and then licked around my lobe, flicking my diamond drop-earrings with her pointed tongue.

"You're good at that." I said and smiled, as I melted. Her breath hot on my ear as she did it again. The lift's upward momentum was slowing. I moved a hand to her breast. I pushed inside her bra to discover a firm, small raspberry-sized nipple finishing her perfect breast. She lifted her hand and gripped mine as I tweaked her nipple. She pulled back from my ear and looked me squarely in the eye without easing her grip. She exhaled and then squeezed my hand even harder.

Fuck! She is so fucking hot. She lifted her other hand, and gently traced around my mouth with her middle finger. The unmistakable aroma of sex — my sex — filled my senses as the lift doors opened. We stepped out and she followed me down the corridor as I opened my clutch to retrieve my room card.

I swiped the card across the door lock. As the light turned green, and I opened the door, I felt her hand slide up the back of my thigh and lift the back of my dress over my ass all the way to my waist. Walking in front of her into the fully lit room, I could see my reflection in the window dead ahead. My legs. My hips. My perfectly hair-free brazilian. And, as I turned into the sitting room … my husband. Sitting with the hi-fi playing softly and pouring himself another glass from a bottle of Johnny Blue.

Cocktails

"Jesus!" I exclaimed loudly, frantically pulling my dress back down.

"Honey," he said. "I think you and your cute little friend here might need to *do* quite a few Hail Mary's."

Once again this evening I found myself momentarily speechless.

He walked to kiss me hello as he explained, "Monday's meeting was cancelled after Johnny had a car accident or something, so there was no reason to stay in Jakarta and work over the weekend. I went straight to the airport and managed to squeeze onto tonight's 6:30pm flight. Got here about ten minutes ago."

"You should have called me," I said.

"Well I tried to but discovered on the plane that I'd packed my phone into my check though bag, so … and then a friend — you've met him, Anson … um, I forget — anyway, he insisted as he was going right past Mongkok. So once his driver had found us, I was here before I knew it."

"And before Karen knew it," added Li Chi still standing where I left her and only now picking her jaw up off the floor.

"I'm sorry I should have introduced … this is my surprising husband, Martin. Martin, this is a friend I met tonight, Li Chi."

"Maybe I should be going."

"You're very welcome to stay, Li Chi," countered Martin. "There's no point rushing off early, you've already racked up the Hail Mary's!" He smiled. "Let me get you both a drink, you both look like … you need one."

As he opened the champagne, I moved back to stand beside her. I took her hand and held it before lifting to kiss her fingers. I turned to her and looked into her eyes, "I really want you to stay … if you're comfortable." Then I kissed her lips. Martin returned with two glasses of champers.

As he turned to get his, she looked at me and asked once more, "Are you sure it's okay?" It was clear she was staying so I turned the lights down, turned the music up and soon we were back to where things were before I'd opened the door.

The three of us — Miss Lychee, Martin and I — were sort of slow dancing and embracing in the sitting room. She excused herself and headed to the powder room. As the door closed, Martin removed my dress completely and immediately on her return, I lifted hers over her

Cocktails

head. We danced and embraced a little more before I took her by the hand, suggesting to Martin over my shoulder, that he join us in the shower. Minutes later, the door opened and Martin walked in. He left the door ajar but turned off the lights. So many soapy hands — all at once, in the dark, it was impossible to know who's were whose. Miss Lychee and I were the first out. When he joined us in the bedroom, I said, "Honey, you can watch but you can't join in … yet."

He sat on the chair in the half-light watching her guiding my head and tongue. I rolled onto my back — my feet pointing towards him. She turned around, straddling my hips, and kissed me on the lips. Finally, I looked at Martin and said, "I think I've got just the job for you, my ever-obedient husband."

Dusty Lane lives north of Sydney near the Hawkesbury River. Writing fills in the gaps between other competing distractions like red wine and work — although the boundaries are very blurry. Almost as blurry as the boundaries between fact and fiction.

Water from the River Ganges
— Rowena Michel

He was larger than life in the melting room. She couldn't help staring at his Neanderthal-like features. His mouth was ripe. He had a protruding forehead and crazy hair. Though he wasn't bony, his carriage was lean with long forearms and thighbones. He moved like an ancient hunter. The most impressive thing about him, she thought, were his hands and his strong fingers and thumbs. One hand was large enough to smother her whole abdomen.

The two men sat cross-legged on a single bed, while she tucked-up bird like, watching from the corner. Although seeming submissive, she was smiling to herself as she pondered the size of other parts of his body.

The sounds of New Delhi wafted in and out of their room. Her boyfriend and his tall guest drank whiskey and smoked cigarettes. The guest sat demurely, mostly listening, but from time to time, he glanced at her. He caught her eye and she smiled. Finally, he suggested they call it a night and let the girl sleep. Until then, her boyfriend hadn't given her a second thought.

Their break-up was imminent. He felt nothing and told her so. At the same time, she clung to threads of hope they wove in bed. One night he had revealed the deepest crevice in his soul. She thought it was because he loved her, but she was wrong. She knew she couldn't survive on his scraps for much longer. Wanting more, she made the decision.

Delhi was their crossroads. It was the night before they were due to go their separate ways. At first she was hurt that her boyfriend had invited a friend to their room on their last night together. But when the intruder bowed his head as he entered their room, she forgot her petty hurt. Sparks were flying, a flame ignited. Perhaps it was mere curiosity, but there was something about him…

After Delhi, she went to Tibet. The decision had been made months before in an act of self-preservation. Busy working in a large school, she felt real again. There were no other foreigners in the district. The locals were suspicious, so she made friends with isolation. Life went on with plugged ears, closed eyes and mouth shut, just as the police had

Cocktails

instructed. Drawing deep, piece by piece, she rebuilt herself and remembered who she was.

Months slowly ticked by. Amidst the majestic beauty of vast grasslands and snow white mountains, her courageous students inspired her to be stronger and fight for her own needs. That's when an unexpected visitor emerged from the corner of her mind. Her memory of him was alive and it came galloping bareback down the mountain, whooping and laughing. Riding swiftly to watch her while she slept.

He was a frequent visitor now. In bed he whispered ancient words in her dreams. She could feel him getting closer. The hooves of his horse pounded, his breathing was heavy. Bare skin on skin flickered through her mind along with images of his large coarse hands folding her softness.

Sleepless nights were filled with fantasies and searching. She imagined fingers tracing circles and felt pulsing, engulfing and swelling. Sometimes on-line, she scoured through countless faces, recommended friends, friends of friends. Always searching.

During another long night of tossing and turning, she opened her laptop in a final attempt to find him. Her hope was dwindling. It was 3am. As time passed, her incessant fantasies had become a curse. The blue light from the screen bounced across her face as she typed his name for the hundredth time. She had tried every possible spelling but her searches had been fruitless.

Suddenly, there he was. She froze when she saw his face on the screen. It was hard to believe that he existed in real life, not just in her dreams. It had been over a year since they met in Delhi. They had shared a few glances and one or two coy smiles, but that was it. Still, her heart was racing.

Holding her breath she typed, "Do you remember me?"

"I could never forget you," he replied. "When are you returning to India?"

It was simple and it was madness. Already on thin ice, another trip away would be testing the patience of her closest friends and family. She never really believed in destiny but she knew she would regret not taking the risk to meet him. She needed to know if he would fill her as she imagined.

Cocktails

The steward informed the passengers that the descent into Delhi had commenced. Her head was swarming. Again and again, she dissected the memory from their brief meeting. She wondered if he would meet her at the airport as he had promised. She knew she was walking the fine line between adventure and stupidity.

The thick, hot air slapped her in the face as she walked through the airport doors into madness. People were yelling, grabbing her bags, offering taxis and hotels. She looked around for him. Amongst the immaculate hair on dark Indian heads, she figured his scraggy locks and towering frame would be easy to spot. Sweat ran down her chest and between her thighs. Her shirt clung to her back as she scanned the crowds.

After a short time she realised he was late. She needed time to clear her mind. She thought of the afternoon heat, entangled together in bed sheets. She turned and wheeled her case back inside the terminal.

She splashed water on her face and looked up. Her reflection seemed warped. Perhaps it was jetlag, perhaps it was doubt. After spraying Chanel on her neck, she suddenly felt nauseous. The fragrance seemed to clash with the clammy air and everything about her seemed out of place. Her bedroom fantasies of him seemed ridiculous here, in the heaving rawness of India, just as ridiculous as her clean cotton blouse and compact laptop.

Calming herself, she again returned to the main gates of the terminal and found a place to sit. In a small tea shop just near the entrance, she drank sweet tea and waited. From there, she could see him arrive without being carried away by the demands of drivers, porters, travellers and thieves.

She waited.

Eventually, a security guard with an oversized moustache approached her. "Madam, you are waiting for someone, no?" he asked.

"Yes," she replied, clearing her husky throat, "he is coming."

"Madam, it is not good for you to sit here for too long. This is Delhi. Can you call your friend?"

"Oh," she stammered. "Yes, I suppose I should."

Not wanting to admit it, two hours had passed and he hadn't come. She carefully unfolded the piece of paper revealing his number and handed it to the security guard.

Cocktails

"Can I use your phone?" she asked.

He dialled the number and listened for a while. Then handing the phone to her he said, "Madam, the number is disconnected. You should find a hotel."

"Thank you," she replied. "Maybe I will wait just a little more. I think he will come soon," she said, trying to look relaxed.

As the guard walked away, she knew he was right. But not wanting to give up hope, she resolved to wait for one more hour. After that, if he still hadn't come, she would find a hotel. First sleep, she thought, then digest all this craziness.

Time moved too fast in that hour. Nerves evaporated into steely cynicism. She cursed herself for her childish, lollipop dreams. There was no such thing as love or destiny, she thought. She glanced around at her surroundings for the first time. This is reality, she thought. Vivid colour, hazy with dust, fermented fumes, friendly smiles amidst poverty and thieving children.

She bought a bottle of water and picked at the label, a picturesque scene of people bathing and drinking pristine water. She read the words around the bottle, "From the snowy mountains of Tibet to the Holy Water of the River Ganges. Revitalise your soul and cleanse your spirit." Twelve hours ago, she would have thought this was a meaningful message, but in that moment, she only scoffed and wiped the sweat from her brow.

The room was dark. The sound of the fan spinning round and round clicked and purred. She must have fallen asleep. Mild panic arose as she tried to recall where she was, what time it was and what had happened. When she remembered, she only felt numb.

The piercing tone of her phone roused her. It was him.

As his words tumbled out, she could make no sense of his ancient language. He spoke too quickly. The distress in his voice was all she heard. He spilled a hundred questions, "Where was she? Was she safe? Did she believe there really had been an accident? Did she believe he was not lying?"

He wanted her to answer but she couldn't. Quiet tears escaped as she was flooded with fatigue and relief. She put the phone down as she heard him say, "Don't go anywhere. I am coming."

Cocktails

He held her so tightly. Almost crushing her, just as she imagined. She heard him inhale her again. Peeling away their layers. He examined her face, her eyes, the freckles on her arms. His face was kinder than she had remembered.

He swept down her length, blazing a trail with his stubble. His hands pressed upon her stomach. She thought in bits and pieces and the fragments were all mixed up: the words on the water bottle; heat and colour; disapproving glances and cigarettes on the window sill. He moved firmly and she exhaled.

The two of them passed the following days in a haze. Slowly sliding from moments of perfect completion to building thirst. Their bodies were yin and yang. One hard, dark and hot, the other soft, white and cool. They arched, grasped and clutched.

Early one morning she was roused by his tender kiss. He pulled her on to him with ease, like he would his favourite jacket. Later, the essence of him broke into a thousand pieces like spices in the air. It peppered the dust of her soul. Never before had she felt this close. They had no words. They had no history. All they had was the present. He looked into her and whispered the words in his own language, then again in broken English…

"I cherish you, deep in my heart."

Rowena Michel is a freelance writer based on the Gold Coast. Although a town planner by trade, she has tried her hand at teaching English, chaperoning celebrities, singing, waitressing, working behind the bar and shopkeeping. Her true passions however, are writing and travelling.

Kiss In The Dark
— Adam Ipsen

All she could see was darkness. A thick length of fabric had stolen her sight. Without her vision, her heart fluttered.

Every single sensation was so much more acute. The battering of the rain outside was riotous. Her inner temperature had risen several degrees and she could feel it radiating out from her trembling body.

Every last shred of clothing had been stripped from her, right down to her socks. Her skin prickled as the air caressed every inch of her skin. With the blindfold on, it was impossible not to focus on the sensations that remained.

Despite her predicament, or perhaps because of it, her dimpled nipples had sprung to attention. They ached with desire and yearned for what they had not felt in far too long — a confident, skilful touch.

She stood, bare and blindfolded, with her hands pressed against her sides. Were her captor's eyes roaming over her creamy skin and watching every goose bump form?

Her captor. Her breath quickened at the thought of him, and her thighs began to quake. She had taken a good, long look at him before the blindfold had been secured. His tall, dark-haired form was a feast for the eyes — one that she had greedily devoured.

She imagined him pacing around her now, clad in nothing but his crotch-hugging underwear. They wrapped tightly around his toned ass, his heavy bulge, and his powerful hips. She bit her lower lip, wondering whether those hips would be put to good use.

A sweet kiss in the dark made her freeze, and in a heartbeat, she returned it. When her captor's warm mouth pulled away, the ghost of the kiss remained, tingling on her own lips.

"From now until I tell you otherwise, you are to forget everything about who you were." His masculine voice was rich and distinctive: a deep baritone with a commanding edge. "Your new name is Isabella, and I am your Master." He paused to savour the word, as if he had sensed the secret delight that had coursed through her. "What's your new name?" he prompted.

Cocktails

"Isabella." The sound of her new name sent a delicious little shiver down her spine. It was a beautiful name — and now it was hers.

"And who am I?"

His commanding tone made her voluptuous body tremble. "My Master," she huskily replied.

A pair of strong hands slipped around her narrow waist and confidently trailed up her soft belly. His hands cupped her pink-tipped peaks from below and squeezed them forcefully.

"Who do these belong to?" he asked, his hot breath caressing the back of her ear. Artful fingers stroked her rosy areolas and coaxed a helpless moan from her lips. Her breasts and nipples had always been extremely sensitive — but were even more so in a pair of hands like his.

"You," Isabella purred. Her breasts belonged to him, as did every other part of her. There were no words for how liberating it felt to give herself over to him, both in body and in soul. No responsibility. No worries. Nothing.

His warm breath heralded the touch of his full lips against her neck. They teased her tender skin, and a carnal moan spilled from her lips. Her legs quaked and threatened to give way at any moment.

"On your knees." Without conscious thought, Isabella obeyed. She dropped down and felt the plush carpet cushioning her knees. She didn't know what to expect, and her heart raced with excitement.

She heard movement and her nose was filled with a heavy masculine scent. The source of the potent musk was barely inches away, and she greedily inhaled its fragrance. "My cock is in front of your face. Worship it with your hands and lips," her master ordered her.

Isabella flushed as she fumbled towards his manhood in the blackness. As soon as her nose bumped against his rigid flesh, she reached forward to lavish it with her affections.

She searched out with her slender fingers, trailing them down his straining shaft to his base. Upon finding her prize, she slid her thumb and index finger around his impressive girth and gently squeezed. Her lips parted again, slowly, as she gave the underside of his bulging cock a long, languid lick, savouring his distinctive taste.

He pressed his throbbing dick against her tongue, urging her to continue. She kissed and suckled on his foreskin; pulling it into her mouth and gently nibbling. Her mouth thoroughly occupied, her hand began to stroke his wonderfully thick cock.

His pleasured groan told her everything she needed to know. "Good girl," he murmured. His powerful fingers stroked the top of her head. She purred against his cock as his fingers slipped through her silky hair.

"Suck it." He broke the silence with his rumbling voice. His powerful fingers pressed her head forward towards his cock.

Isabella swooned as she obediently parted her lips around his shaft. She took in as much of it as she could. She could feel his cock twitching between her fingers, and she felt a fluttering of pride, knowing that she was pleasing him.

Her mouth filled as she sucked on his hardness, her wet lips sliding back and forth along his pulsing length. She was blindfolded, butt-naked, and servicing his cock, and she loved every minute of it.

"Stop." Her master commanded her after a time. Isabella was worried that she had done something wrong, but her fears were immediately allayed. "I have other plans for you. Stand up and follow me."

His authoritative tone and the lingering taste of his cock on her lips intensified the broiling heat between her thighs. She stood up. Strong, powerful hands grabbed her wrists and led her through the darkness. She felt the impossibly smooth touch of silk bed sheets against her lower legs. "Up on the bed."

She obediently crawled on to the yielding mattress. Led by his guiding hands, she moved across the bed, arms and legs sinking into the softness until her hands were lifted and placed upon a stiff headboard. She breathlessly wondered what her master had in mind.

She felt the wrapping of cuffs around her wrists, and a clinking of metal anchoring them in place. Now on her knees and with her arms secured to the headboard, Isabella felt a deep sense of arousal. She trusted her master with her life, and had no problems putting herself at his mercy.

"Every kiss you feel, and every little mark I leave on your beautiful body is a sign of my love, Isabella. I am marking you as mine, and no one else's," he growled possessively.

Her heart fluttered at his forceful tone. She wanted nothing more than to be claimed by him. "Please mark me, Master. Do whatever you

Cocktails

want to me." She begged. She arched her back like a cat and poked her aching ass outwards towards her master, eager for more. There was only the moment, and in that moment all that existed was her, her master, and what was happening to her.

There was another kiss in the dark — this time on her milky back. She moaned as a shower of sensual kisses rained down on her spine and travelled towards her rump. It was the most delicious kind of downfall, and it ended at the cleft of her shapely ass.

A single touch between her legs sent an electric thrill up her spine. She arched her back as the tip of his dick slid softly against her slick mound. She let out a sharp gasp, contrasting his low rumble. Her first instinct was to thrust back with her hips, eager to please him, but strong hands on her rounded cheeks controlled her movements. Instead, his hardness ran along the length of her sex, from bottom to top, then back down again, over and over and over. He built a steady rhythm, a pulsing tide of pleasure that rippled through her.

Just as her whole body threatened to give way, overwhelmed with sensation, she felt the press of his powerful hips and his cock eased inside of her. Inch by inch, she felt his shaft slide into her, and with every push of his hips, she sunk further into ecstasy.

She cried out with pleasure as his length caressed her inner walls. She rocked against him in unconscious rhythm, clenching his cock. She began to lose track of time as he had his way with her helpless body.

She felt him pulse and give one last forceful thrust. Buried in her deepest depths, his hot seed spurted and spilled inside her. The coiled sensation in her abdomen reached its peak and with a shuddering moan, they climaxed together.

Her body collapsed against the sheets, but she was only dimly aware of this, adrift in a sea of delight. Hazily, she recalled a blanket being wrapped around her, her cuffs being removed, and her blindfold being removed. As she regained some sense of self, she found herself with her head nuzzled into the crook of her master's neck.

"... Master?" she timidly whispered, wondering how long she had lost herself in bliss. Calming fingers stroked the top of her head and she was pulled into a tight embrace.

Cocktails

"You've been away for a while, my love," her master told her in soothing tones. She snuggled against him, feeling completely at peace. "I'm so glad we tried that out. That was ... I mean... it was absolutely amazing," she purred. She'd never climaxed so hard in her entire life.

She burrowed into her beloved husband's arms and drifted off. As she fell into the shoals of sleep, she dreamed of kisses in the dark.

Adam Ipsen lives, sleeps, and breathes writing. A former print journalist, aspiring author, and incurable geek, he lives in the Latrobe Valley with his lovely wife and editor, Sharon, who finds the clickety-clack of his keyboard soothing. His works are highly inspired by Anne McCaffrey and Neil Gaiman.

Hangman's Blood
— Maria Bonar

I was but moments from having my life extinguished. The noose dangled before me, while my brother, Hamish, already swung from the branch on my right, his feet slowly turning in the early morning chill. He would never more steal a fat lamb from the Laird's flock.

I shook with terror and grief. As I stammered a last prayer, my legs failed me. I would have fallen from the granite boulder on which I stood but for Douglas McBarran, the Gillie, willingly acting as hangman this day. He dragged me upright once more. His stink filled my nostrils as he clasped me from behind, the dagger at his waist pressing painfully into my back. He thrust his other hand under my skirts.

"Such a pity to waste this sweet young flesh, lads. What say ye?" he rasped, pulling me round to face him.

Perhaps it was this final indignity that sparked a swift flame of defiance in my belly. McBarran and his men had neglected to truss me as they had my brother. I seized his dagger and plunged it into his black heart before the thought had properly seeded and bloomed in my mind. We fell together behind the rock, McBarran's blood spraying over me, the coppery taste foul on my lips.

How a spirit at its lowest ebb can suddenly blaze like a forest fire, leaping from tree to tree! I fled through Kirkmaiden Woods panting like an animal. The path led me back to the clearing where the four horses were tethered. My icy fingers could scarcely untie the reins. Mounting the nearest horse, I urged him to a gallop, the other three following closely behind. Once away from the woods, I spied the smoke from our chimney, still curling peacefully upwards as though nought had happened since Hamish and I were so rudely snatched from our hearth.

Yarding the horses, I closed the gate behind me and ran to the pump, washing the hangman's blood from my face before entering the cottage. I stripped off my soiled kirtle and hastily donned Hamish's trousers and shirt before bundling some food and clothing into a sack.

Prising a loose brick from my hidey-hole in the inglenook, I removed my treasures; a silver betrothal ring, my mother's brooch and two

Cocktails

pennies. Pocketing them and tucking my hair into Hamish's cap, I was ready to leave.

I rode like the west wind for the next hour, the other horses galloping behind me. When I reached the crossroads I tethered McBarran's stallion and searched the other horses' saddlebags, helping myself to a finely wrought knife, some food and a few coins. McBarran's saddlebag held a leather pouch containing three sovereigns — riches indeed. I led the spare horses back the way they had come, slapping the leading mare's rump and urging them homewards. I had no wish to give the Laird's men further reason to hunt me down. McBarran's horse I would keep. I headed north-west, to Ballantrae, the harbour town of my birth.

I cantered steadily onwards, quietly skirting villages on the way. My escape from the noose caused me to savour the glory of that clear spring day. The scent of bluebells in the woods, a bumblebee heavy with pollen droning past my ear and the song of the fast flowing stream skipping over the rocks.

As I neared Ballantrae, I decided I would seek help from Ross McKenzie. *He owes me a debt,* I thought sourly. Ross, who pledged his love to me when I was seventeen, then betrayed me with Morag, once my dearest friend.

Ross had told me, "When I finish my apprenticeship with the blacksmith and can afford to keep a wife, we will wed."

In the meantime, we met secretly in the woods, where he covered me with kisses. He explored my body as though it were a foreign land, full of exotic enchantments. I allowed him to discover, but not to conquer. I was ever mindful to keep my precious maidenhead intact, for a deflowered maid risks abandonment and bleak spinsterhood.

As I rode the stallion along the track, I grew lusty with memories of those secret trysts. I tightened my legs around the saddle, gripping harder, breathing faster, my juices flowing. How I longed for another taste of those forbidden fruits.

My father, the clan Chieftain, looked down on Ross and his family. He had other plans for me. He would marry me off to old Sir Alexander McLeod to strengthen his alliances in the north. When my father and my two eldest brothers were slain while fighting alongside Robert the Bruce, my mother, Hamish and I fled south.

Cocktails

I had scarcely been away a month when Morag seduced Ross. Another month later she told him she was carrying his bairn. They were swiftly wed, but she tricked him as she tricked me, for their son was born ten months after the wedding. Bitterness rose up in me like gall, when I brooded on her treachery.

How fortunes change. I lost half my family, my sweetheart and my dear friend in that one dark season. Sir Alexander found another young maiden to marry. My mother died of a fever soon afterwards, the cruellest loss.

I rode on. When I finally reached Ballantrae, I dismounted, tethering the horse to a tree a little way behind the smithy. My bitterness melted away when I saw Ross at the forge. I watched him from the shadows for a time, making sure he was alone before whistling a low note. He stopped hammering and looked up. I signalled to him, as I had done so many times in the past. He laid down his tools and hurried towards me.

"Rhona! What brings you here?"

He moved to embrace me, before remembering he was a married man. I told him of Hamish's misfortune and my own timely escape from the noose.

"I need to outrun the Laird's men, so I plan to sail to the Western Isles. I have some kin there, on my mother's side. Will you help me arrange safe passage?" I asked him.

He nodded. "Ewan McDonald is here from Islay. I believe he sails tomorrow."

"I have a horse to sell. I can pay him." I added.

Ross inspected the stallion, running a hand over his flanks. "I will take the horse to Ewan and ask him if he is willing."

"Thank you."

"Morag is away visiting her sister. You can stay with me tonight," he said, looking away as I caught a spark of desire in his eyes.

He led me to the cottage behind the smithy, before leaving with the horse. I bathed and dressed in my petticoat, and nought else. I looked over the cottage, spying in every corner, disdainfully handling Morag's belongings. I rummaged in her sewing box. Using her embroidery scissors, I snipped a long curl from my red hair, plaiting it around the silver betrothal ring Ross had given me when he first pledged his love.

Cocktails

Morag would surely recognise it. I hid it in her sewing box, my vengeful message to her.

I helped myself to some cider while waiting for Ross. I confess I drank more than I should have. When he returned, I was rosy with desire.

"Ewan will buy the horse. He sails tomorrow," he said, eying my breasts through the thin petticoat.

I embraced him, inhaling his once familiar manly smell. "Thank you, Ross." I murmured, my lips on his neck.

He carried me straight to bed. I closed my eyes and opened my mouth to his deep, slow kisses. He whispered coarse words in my ear, telling me how he would pleasure me with fingers, tongue and cock before the night was over. A shock of desire shot through me. I kissed him back wantonly, my nipples rising against the thick, dark hair on his chest. His cock poked my thighs, so I kept my legs tightly closed, lest he forget and breach my slippery maidenhead.

While his fingers delicately stroked, teased and explored, he kissed the palm of my hand. He circled his tongue around my nipples, then on the soft inner curve of my elbow. He slowly moved southwards, trailing kisses and probing all my hidden nooks. He reached my ankles, his warm hands fondling my foot while his tongue pushed between my toes. Such bliss!

Aroused, I hungered for the taste and scent of his cock. Only when it was safely in my mouth, did I open my secret place to him. His beard ravished my thighs as he lapped up my nectar, making me gasp with anticipation. My lips and tongue greeted his taut, satiny roundness as a dear friend after a long absence. The silkiness of his skin belied the underlying iron. While I caressed and gorged on him, his thumbs spread open my secret place revealing my hidden rosebud, which he nibbled with exquisite deftness. A deep tingling surged through my belly, but subsided as he teased me, withdrawing his tongue, then slowly circling his mouth back towards my secret place. His fingers brushed only lightly over my fiery centre. I squirmed, pleading for more. For harder, rougher fondling.

Abruptly, he rolled me on my back, his powerful hands gripping my ankles, dragging me to the very edge of the mattress. I resisted as he tried

Cocktails

to spread my thighs, fearful he would force his cock in and ruin me, giving me more hardness than I bargained for. Instead, he knelt beside the bed. He eased his right hand under me, his thumb sliding tightly into my secret place, his middle finger stroking and circling my derriere. With his left hand, he fingered my rosebud, spreading it open. He pushed his tongue deep between my clenched and trembling thighs until a maelstrom of delight swept me away.

I pleasured him again, sucking his cock, tasting his yeasty sap when he shot his bolt. I relished the thought that we could lie together this long night feasting on each other, lips glistening. And we did. Come morning, my nipples and rosebud were tender and swollen from all Ross' attentions, but my maidenhead remained intact. Perhaps a little stretched.

What joy to wake on the wings of the morning from a luscious dream, to find the dream is born of reality; my lover's tongue already rousing my secret place. We breakfasted on lust alone until it was time to dress and depart.

I realised I would not see Ross again. The corrosive bitterness I had held in my heart towards him had vanished. I wished him well. I reclaimed the betrothal ring from the sewing box, concealing it in my pocket. I would leave him only sweet memories and the scent of my secret place on his fingertips.

*Scots born, **Maria Bonar** lives in Perth, Western Australia. Now retired from management and research roles in the corrections and health fields, she writes short fiction, articles and the occasional poem. She is currently the vice president and newsletter editor of the* Society of Women Writers WA.

Hot Carl Msagro
— Diana Thurbon

I'm not a virgin. I'm almost seventeen, but I look older. My name is Julie. I have a nice figure, a golden tan and pretty blue eyes. My friends say I look nineteen or twenty. I always wear makeup and I keep my nails polished in sexy reds. My long straight blonde hair is clean and glossy. Boys — and men — come onto me. I'd done it with six different boys — each experience worse than the one before. I could describe them and what they did, or more likely didn't do. You'd be bored like me. By number six I could fake a pretty good orgasm which I used every time to end the whole pointless experience.

I won't describe them in detail though; you'd only be grossed out by descriptions of little dribbly dicks and boys who thought foreplay was pinching my tender pink nipples — hard. Or sucking on them — hard! Two of them came before they could get my frilly pink knickers off. I ended up with their sticky warm cum all over me. And nothing happened for me. Just a zero. I'm hoping for sex with passion — even love.

Yet though I am experienced sexually, Carl Msagro is turning my world upside down. He recently started in the pizza bistro where I work after school. We both cook. That means we touch and brush against each other in the too small kitchen. The first time I accidently touched his hand the room actually spun round me.

If you read a book and the writer says 'the room spun' and you think it's a stupid cliché; it is actually not. I know because it did truthfully happen to me the first time our hands touched. When I could see straight again I looked at him with that Princess Diana look I'd practised. My dark blue eyes looking up through my long eyelashes at his even longer eyelashes, I was sure I must look vulnerable and tempting — a sort of apple in Eden — fresh, a bit crunchy and ready for plucking.

He *must* have noticed the current that had run through my hand when we'd touched. Yet he didn't even look at me. He was chopping garlic. I realised for him, *nothing* had happened. The second time was pretty much the same as the first; only difference was he was chopping capsicums. The third time didn't have any chopping, we were

Cocktails

squeezing past each other in the pantry and my breasts were pushed against his back. I could feel them swell and my nipples become hard and pointy. Oh God! The room didn't spin but I felt a rush of cream come out of my pussy and my panties felt all wet, my face flushed red and I could feel my nipples growing even harder. My stomach was churning. When I had recovered a bit, I surreptitiously looked at my hot Carl for a sign; just some acknowledgement that he had at least felt — *something*.

Again, nothing. He is older than me perhaps he thinks I'm too young to be interested in sex. Huh, sex with my super hot dish Carl was *all* I could think about; besides people do say I look older. Perhaps he was in love with another girl and was trying to be faithful. I desperately needed to spark his interest — make his dick blush and grow hard and stiff — at least.

The last time we touched was yesterday. I tripped over the scraps bin. I was looking at where I figured his prick would be under his apron, instead of where I was going. I landed in a heap on the concrete floor. I had a small cut on my shin where I had made contact with the bin. Hot Carl pulled me up. My face came right up near his. My lips parted and the now familiar wet feeling flooded the crotch of my panties. I was breathing hard and fast, I imagined I could see the bulge in the front of his whites. I could have imagined it.

He looked at me with concern. Are you all right? Did you get a fright? Your pulse is racing, I can see it in your throat, you are almost panting, and your face is flushed. Are you hurt?"

Am I hurt? Oh boy. "No I'm not hurt ... just a scratch on my knee."

Carl reached down into the cupboard, then standing up he handed me the first aid kit and went back to mixing dough fast as if to make up time he'd had to waste helping me. I felt devastated. My knickers were soaked. I desperately needed to bring myself off. He was obviously blind. I was in the flower of my womanhood and he had no interest in deflowering me. Of course that had effectively already been done, but he couldn't know that, could he!

That night finally alone in my bed and able to bring myself to orgasm I filled my mind with memories of his scent, the feel of his touch, as I masturbated, massaging faster and faster round my clitoris I imagined

Cocktails

I was massaging his cock and I came and came and came. I couldn't stop myself. I kept going so long I rubbed the side of my clit raw. Pretty dumb. I was so wet down there I hadn't thought I would need any lubricant. Once when I came it was like I was peeing and I made sucking noises with my vagina as I imagined sucking him in and squeezing his cock tight against the sides of my narrow, tunnel. Wet cream, mixed with more wet, I could feel my heart pounding as it raced, skipped beats and I got hotter and hotter and threw the covers off. I slipped down on to the floor and watched myself in the mirror — OOOH ... Now I knew what a real orgasm could feel like. Strictly speaking more like six real orgasms in a row.

In the end I'd sneaked downstairs and nicked a bag of frozen peas, to hold on my poor hot bruised and raw fanny. It took a long time to cool down. I wanted to go all over again; Carl had me so hot, but I stopped myself before I was unable to walk in the morning. I had gazed longingly at the zucchinis in the fridge when I opened the freezer for the peas. I'd been strong and left the substitute cocks where they were.

I decided I must be in love; I had to seduce Carl. I determined to make him jealous; surely I could stir his loins as they say in the romance books.

This morning I spent a long time in the bathroom expertly doing my eyes and using my straightener on my hair. I pulled on my best super soft blue cashmere sweater. It matched my eyes. I wore heeled boots and carried my flats for work. As I entered Carl looked up.

"Hi Honey you're all dressed up today?"

The 'Honey' was enough, he had a beautiful deep throaty voice. I felt myself creaming my pants again. "I have a date after work, Carl."

"Oh really, so do I."

I couldn't wait to see my competition. I was so nervous I got very clumsy and we touched so often I decided I needed to bring spare panties to work from now on.

Finally the end of our shift approached. I took off my whites and changed into my sexy high-heeled boots.

I noticed a bright yellow Monaro sports pull in; right out the front of the bistro. That's against the law bitch, I thought silently. I was stirred up waiting to see her. The car door opened; a very tall middle-aged

Cocktails

George Clooney look alike, unfolded onto the road. He walked toward the shop door as I gazed in awe.

"Hi Carl are you ready? The party is waiting for you."

I watched them leave — hand in hand. My belly fell down, past my bum, and into my sexy boots. Watching Hot Carl Msagro leave with his boyfriend I couldn't help wondering if the zucchinis in the fridge were still nice and firm.

Diana Thurbon lives in Melbourne with a husband and three dogs. Known at home for her cooking; all would probably be astounded to read this story. Diana has been writing short stories for six years — ever since her first writing competition entry won the first prize. Not as dramatically successful since, she nevertheless really hopes you enjoy reading this, her first ever erotic story.

Satin Sheets
— Michael Wilkinson

His secretary sashayed across the marble floor, looked at Stella with barely contained contempt and said in a husky voice, "The Minister is waiting for you. Follow me, please."
Stella felt like telling him that his belly ring was just 'so yesterday,' but held her tongue. More and more often she was thinking just like the people she was employed to protect the community against. *I must be getting old.*
The Minister, Anthony Priest, was just as flash in person as he was on the vids. A thin, taut face. *How many face-lifts?* Perfect nails, skin soft as angora jumper and bright red pants that were sprayed on, showing every taut muscle and his large penis, that he was, oddly, wearing to the left. *What's his game? Is he trying to intimidate me? I reckon he's wearing contour undies! I'll know in a second.* She stifled a laugh.
"Minister, so glad to meet you." Stella walked over and stood legs slightly apart while the minister felt her through her Koton undies. She had placed a Vagil Moisture Pad over her vulva that morning, knowing the Minister would go through the entire greeting ritual. After a few seconds he removed his hand, sniffed his middle finger and gave a little bow. With an inward sigh, Stella grasped the outline of penis and gave it three squeezes. Again she nearly laughed as it steadily increased in size by nearly a third. They were contour undies, and expensive ones at that. *Must be the Alpha 4S. He's such a prick.*
When Stella had first started as Director of Procreation she had entertained, briefly, the banning in the Department of the wearing of contour undies, vagil moisture pads, belly rings, labia projectors, transparent ballsacs and all the other ridiculous sexual paraphernalia, but when she raised it with her Deputy, who had been in the Department for several years, he cautioned her against it. "Recruitment is hard enough, Stella, without making us freaks." She had rapidly shelved that idea. *Shame I kept the status quo, I'm so sick of having a damp crotch. The bloody vagil pad is leaking again.* Stella sat down on the deep

Cocktails

leather chair and carefully arranged her legs so Priest had a good look up her microskirt to the damp patch forming between her legs.

He in turn sat opposite her, legs splayed wide, allowing her an uninterrupted view of his throbbing cock through his latexon. *Yes, as I thought. An Alpha 4S with a Pinktooth enabled vibrahead.*

"Now Stella, do you want sex before we start?"

"That's a very kind offer, Minister, I can see you find me attractive and as you have felt from my really wet pussy, I would love to bed you immediately, but given the time, I think it would be best if we pushed on." *God, I hate this formal small talk. Doesn't he know why I'm here and what I am about to tell him? He's just as vacuous as the rest of the Government.*

"I do have some incredibly good Lubagel if you are feeling a bit dry." He looked directly at her, as he insulted her. Stella felt bit surprised at his animosity. Her Deputy had warned her that Priest was known for his power games but she had always harboured a thought that he would be reasonably normal towards the public service. After all the public service existed to serve and service the Ministers. *We're all on the same side, you bastard.*

"No, no, Minister. I'm slick and ready to go. Your penis looks delicious. I'm just holding back as I'm aware that you're meeting a delegation from the Sydney Catholic Seminary next, and I don't want to exhaust you." Stella caught the stifled smirk of the flunky in the corner. *Checkmate, Tony, you fuck.*

"Oh, I think I can handle them," smiled the Minister, giving a tight smile. "Yes, you're probably right about the time. Please brief me... Stella."

Thank goodness, now we can get on.

"As Minister for Population Enhancement you would be well aware that our birth rate has fallen well below replacement rate and in twenty years it is expected that there won't be nearly enough humans to repair the carebots and our entire eldercare program will fail." Stella was on comfortable ground now. She had given this talk to the last five Ministers over the last three years. But none of them took action. *Too busy being a dysfunctional, faction-ridden Government to care about the future of humankind.*

Cocktails

"But our policies have *all* been about enhancing the birth rate," interrupted the Minister. "We've sexualised everything. Facebook is wall-to-wall porn. Sexting is taught in schools. ID photos are all taken naked. We've banned X-rays at airports and returned to full body strip searches — admittedly that has slowed things down a bit. Everyone gets their clothes mixed up." He laughed. "We've gone fully Greek and all our sporting events are in the buff. What is left to do? What is left to the imagination? Nothing!"

"Precisely, Minister." Stella paused. She liked this part of the briefing. She always hoped that suddenly they would get it. She was always disappointed. She didn't imagine that Tony would get it either. She had a bet on with her Deputy.

"I guess we could lower the age of consent to twelve. Try banning contraception again?"

She'd won her bet. Again. "No Minister, I'm sorry but you have already given the answer."

"I have?" He looked a bit confused. *Gormless git.*

"Yes, Minister. You said that 'Nothing is left to the imagination.'"

"That's just the point! There is nothing left to do!"

Calm down. You could try listening instead of talking. Time for the soft soap.

"But Minister, you have given the answer. You have told us what to do. Quite masterfully, if I may say so." And with that comment she leant over and gave his penis, or rather his *Alpha 4S*, a squeeze.

"Oh yes? What?"

"Do you know where orgasms come from?"

"Are you trying to patronise me?"

"No Minister, it was a legitimate question." *Oh do get over the power games, Tony. Can't we have civilised conversation?*

"Our sex organs. My penis, your vagina, vulva, clit, G-spot, breasts, whatever. Why do women have so many erogenous zones and we have just one?"

Because your brains aren't big enough to cope with more than a penis. Oh Stella, don't bring it down to his level.

"Minister, orgasms take place in our heads, not our sex organs."

"But..."

Cocktails

Keep going girl. Don't let him start. "...brain scans show that it is our brains that create the orgasms. It's a bit like a light going on. For example, the penis, or the pussy or whatever, is the switch, but it is the brain that is the light bulb. It is the brain that creates the fantasies and frankly our brains are completely dulled, bored and stultified by naked humans. Here, let me show you a vid."

Stella pointed her vidP at the room's main projector. A slightly pixelated image showed on the screen. "Sorry for the quality, Minister, it was shot in 2010. This is a nudist camp. Observe the men. As you can see, all the young women are playing volleyball and they aren't wearing a thing. What size are the mens' erections?"

"They're just suffering flop. This was before e-viagra of course."

"No Minister, that's the point. Familiarity breeds boredom. The girl's bodies are beautiful. The men are beautiful, but because nakedness in this context is absolutely normal, there is no sexual frisson."

"And that's why we invented e-viagra," said the Minister in a bored voice.

"But Minister, e-viagra is only useful once the man *wants* sex. Because sex is everywhere, he doesn't want sex. No sex, no babies. Falling birth rate. Cause and effect. Simple." Stella finished the last bit in a rush. She could see that the Minister's attention span was at an end.

"Look, Stella, I don't mean to be rude, but my penis is drooping and you're no longer turning me on. You're speaking drivel. We know that plenty of porn is what men and *real* women want and frankly, I need to see the Catholics shortly. Sharpen up your presentation so it can be read it in one minute and email it to my secretary. He can synthesise it into a microbrief. Get it to me by next week. Goodbye." He scratched his groin in dismissal. The Secretary, with a flounce and a wave of his penis sheath closed the door behind her.

"How did it go, Stella?" asked Darcy, her Deputy, as she stormed into the room.

"Why are you still here? The office closed hours ago. Haven't you got a home to go to?" *Oh, it's nice to see you Darcy. Some sanity in a world gone mad.*

Cocktails

"I thought you might like to debrief a bit. I know how tough the briefings can go. I've poured you a chilled Nigerian sauvignon blanc. Boko 2071."

"You sweetie! Well, in short, just as expected. I won our bet. Priest wants it all in a microbrief. Ten years of research in thirty seconds…"

"Well, that's the twenty-fifty generation for you. No concentration."

Stella stared, suddenly noticing her Deputy. "What the hell are you wearing?"

"Just a suit. I did have trouble tying the bowtie, but I think I've worked it out. Pretty dapper, don't you reckon?" He smiled. "Come into the labs, I've got something to show you."

"What?"

"Just come. I ordered it months ago for an experiment and it's just arrived." He placed his hand gently into hers and gave it a squeeze. She followed him, watching how his bottom moved in the crisp, pin-striped trousers — which didn't show every muscle. With a dramatic pause, Darcy grasped the handle and then flung open the wood-panelled door to the lab.

"Good God, Darcy, where did you find a four-poster bed? I've only seen them on pVids."

"I'm told they can be quite comfortable," said Darcy with a smile. "The curtains provide quite some discretion and to cap it all off, I've brought you a…"

"…negligee," finished Stella. "Is there a little red dress on the bed too? Err… without the cutout for the belly-ring?"

"Of course."

"Those sheets. Are they made from sexywarm?"

"No, they're simply satin sheets."

She couldn't quite believe the warm, inviting scene in front of her. "Is that a *real* candle? Not a flickerLED?"

"I like the fragrance and when you blow it out, it's quite something."

"You haven't sprayed the room with pherosex."

"No need," replied Darcy, nibbling her neck and breathing in her scent.

"What porn, have you chosen for us to watch?"

"Nothing."

Cocktails

"Nothing at all?"

"I have this little book of Shakespearean sonnets I'd like to share with you."

Stella kissed him... deeply.

Michael Wilkinson is an Australian writer with a love of the bush. He has been writing since the age of twelve and now, three and a half decades later is still writing. He writes both fiction and non-fiction. He has been published in twelve Stringybark Stories anthologies, including the three erotic fiction collections: The Heat Wave of '76, Between the Sheets *and* Valentine's Day.

Soixante-Neuf
— Julie Davies

"Honest to goodness, Sir. I don't know why you spend so much time teaching visible speech to these deaf strangers. They obviously get by fine with lip reading," said Tom, as he adjusted the wiring he was stringing between the office and laboratory.

"Aye, but if I can help them to communicate more effectively, the way my family can, it will make an enormous difference to their lives," Aleck said. "They need not be so isolated."

"But today of all days, when we're testing the device. Why didn't you postpone their appointment?"

Aleck looked a touch discomposed at this challenge from his underling. He had not yet adjusted to such colonial impertinence, so it was several seconds before he responded.

"The circus is only in Boston for another week. This is the last time I will be able to meet with them and we have made great progress already."

"Tell me, do you think I should adjust the pitch a wee bit higher?"

"Let's just give it a try, shall we," replied Tom, feeling impatient and edgy. "What do you want me to do with them?"

"Do with what?"

"The two acrobatic ladies from PT Barnum's, of course. It's freezing cold in the ante-room."

"Och aye, the ladies. Perhaps we could put them in Mabel's reading alcove. The fires either side should have warmed the air in there too, by now."

Tom sighed. His employer was a good man and a superb inventor but not particularly competent with the mundane details of life. He'd never have made it this far without Tom's practical good sense, no doubt about it.

He walked into the frigid ante-room, smiled with deep insincerity at the two girls, and gestured for them to follow. They signed to each other, before standing. He thought that was a mite rude, rather like guests conversing in a foreign language, until he remembered they had no other way to communicate. Eternally silent women. He rather liked that notion.

Cocktails

Tom stepped aside after opening the door and watched the two lithe young women precede him into the hallway. The Asian girl had a sweet face but kept her eyes modestly downcast as she moved past. The blond had a cheeky grin on her face, as she arched her brows and gave the hip nearest to Tom an exaggerated wiggle.

Bold little monkey. Obviously looking for a bit of fun. She'd no doubt have strong thigh muscles, what with all that dancing and tumbling and suchlike, thought Tom, unable to keep his eyes off her retreating, swaying rear. His stomach clenched.

Ushering them into the alcove between Aleck's office and the laboratory, he retreated back to the lab, where a square metal device lay on the bench; whether full of promise or another failure he didn't yet know.

So much rode on this experiment. Tom desperately wanted to start his own business but he didn't have any capital behind him. Aleck had promised him he'd be on the patent application and share any subsequent royalties, if they could get the damned thing to work.

Time dragged as he watched Aleck make final adjustments, marching back and forth between an identical device in his office and the lab; fussing unnecessarily, in Tom's opinion. He began to feel sleepy from the mesmerising flicker of the fire and the warm fug in the room. He waited for the call, and waited, and waited. His chin dropped onto his chest and soon he was snoring quietly.

They were women of action and they were restless, these two fit young acrobats. How long would the scientist man be? He'd forgotten them for sure. Most people overlooked anyone who wasn't whole. They were used to it.

Neither woman could read, so they paced restlessly back and forth, ignoring the piles of books crammed into every corner of the alcove. Veronica stopped at the small window and looked out into the street. She saw two dogs mating just outside the fence. She laughed and gestured for Mei-Lin to come and see.

They watched until the dogs completed their urgent task and then had wandered away indifferently, as though they'd never even noticed each other. That was how men had always treated the two deaf-mutes, despite their beauty, so they soon found solace — and much better loving — with each other.

They collided as they turned from the window and both raised their hands to steady the other. They looked deeply into each other's eyes, before Veronica turned and opened the door, gazing along the empty corridor. She removed the ornate brass key from the lock and re-closed the door. She shook her head to indicate no-one was about and raised one eyebrow in question. Mei-Lin smiled and brought up her hand to caress Veronica's face. Veronica swiftly locked the door from the inside and turned her head to kiss Mei-Lin's palm, before sweeping her into an embrace.

Mei-Lin ran her tongue along Veronica's upper lip. She could taste the faint sweetness of her lover's skin and goose bumps raised on her own in response. Veronica nibbled at Mei-Lin's lower lip, as her hands slid inside the top of her bodice. She tweaked one nipple and felt Mei-Lin's sharp intake of breath. Her nipples were her on-switch.

In one swift movement, Veronica broke away, bent over and raised the edge of Mei-Lin's gown to her waist. Mei-Lin wriggled out of her bloomers, leaving her corset in place, dark-nippled breasts winking over the top of her bodice.

Veronica pushed her back against the embroidered chaise-longue and knelt between her legs. Mei-Lin began massaging her own breasts, as she arched her head backward over the carved wooden scroll decorating the back of the settee.

Tom didn't know what had awoken him but he was relieved it hadn't been the boss. He snatched up the handpiece to see if Aleck was trying to contact him. He raised it to his ear, but quickly dropped the device, staring in astonishment for a few seconds, before bringing it back up and listening intently. He was riveted to the spot. So were the buttons on his fly, standing out like a juggler's plate balanced on a stick.

Aleck was in a state of high anxiety. So many trials and so many failures. Someone else would beat him to it. He raised the handpiece to his ear. All he could hear was a strange, absence of sound, an echo in an empty chamber. But then a little whispering hiss, like silk rubbing.

Cocktails

A giggle. What in God's name was this?

Rustling. Heavy breathing. Another giggle. Aleck finally realised the junction box he'd installed in the alcove to link the devices in office and laboratory was somehow picking up the sounds in there. He knew exactly what they were doing. An erection tented his trousers as he listened to the two girls making whoopee.

His vivid inventor's imagination went into overtime. What did those who indulged in the practices of Lesbos actually do? They lacked the correct equipment. He concluded they must use their hands to pleasure each other at the same time. Oh my, and possibly their tongues! He instantly envisaged the girls in a *soixante-neuf* position, heads bobbing up and down. Perhaps one was swinging upside down from the candelabra while the other munched, or was he confusing acrobats with trapeze artists?

Aleck leaned forward and pressed his cock up against the back of the chair but it didn't relieve his tension. He swapped the handpiece to his left hand and reached down to rub the full length of his tumescence through the heavy fabric, giving his balls a wee squeeze too. It still wasn't enough. With a soft moan of mixed resignation and shame, he opened his trousers.

Veronica made long, firm licks along Mei-Lin's lips, darting back and forth to the button, feeling it swell under her tongue. Her own pussy began gently oozing love juice. She parted her legs and pressed her crotch against Mei-Lin's lower leg.

Mei-Lin arched her foot and began moving it back and forth to pleasure her lover through her clothing. But she became distracted as her own climax began to build and she stopped. Veronica wasn't going to have that. She pulled back from Mei-Lin, stood a little unsteadily, and quickly stripped off her own bodice and pantaloons. She coaxed Mei-Lin lengthwise onto the chaise-longue and lay on top of her in the reverse direction, one thigh on either side of her face. She arched her back, swaying her shoulders back and forth so her erect nipples would brush against Mei-Lin, as she continued licking. She ignored the jabs of the whalebone at the edges of her corset.

Mei-Lin plunged two fingers into the cavern yawning inches from her face, stroking in and out, as she lapped at Veronica's swollen pussy.

Cocktails

Of course, neither could hear their groans as they got closer and closer to their joint destination. They couldn't know they sounded like baboons claiming territory.

Hesitant footsteps approached the office door. Aleck panicked. He would be caught defiling himself. The shame would be overwhelming. He fumbled with the closure device in the front of his trousers, ripping it upward in fear and haste.

His magnificent erection proved too much for the limited space left inside his trousers. The closure snagged, capturing a large piece of foreskin. Excruciating pain exploded inward. He tried tugging the closure device back down. That hurt even more. His eyes filled with tears of humiliation and agony. He could no longer see what he was doing.

A knock on the door and a near-unintelligible Glaswegian voice burred:

"Mr Bell, would ye like me tae see tae the fire, sirruh?"

He managed a strangled: "No, no, everything is fine, thank you Shelagh," and held his breath, sweat breaking out on his forehead.

Aleck heard the maid's footsteps retreating. He panted with relief but the motion tore his trapped skin, large drops of blood oozing onto his longjohns. He could see why Mr Howe had failed to seriously market his revolutionary patented trouser closer. It was a danger to a man's wellbeing, indeed to his future. But he knew he needed help. He wouldn't be able to extricate himself from this predicament unaided.

Hands shaking, Aleck retrieved the handset he had discarded in a panic and said in as firm a voice as he could manage:

"Mister Watson, come here. I want to see you ..."

Thus it was that Mister Alexander Graham Bell and his colleague, Mister Thomas A. Watson, invented the acoustic telegraph, later known as the telephone, and phone sex on the very same day.

Cocktails

Julie Davies *is a novelist and short story writer from Central Queensland. She has had ten stories published in nine Stringybark anthologies, her latest in* Valentine's Day, *and twenty-five published in other anthologies, literary journals and online magazines. She'll continue writing short stories to motivate herself while she reels from the rejections of her first (non-erotic) novel and struggles with the second. This story is one of an erotic collection she is writing on the deadliest sin through the ages.*

In the Saddle
— R.L. Phoenix

"Like what you see, Darling?"

God that voice. Her whole body shuddered slightly as it flowed over her like melted chocolate. A sensation that ran the length of her body and ended in her pussy. She had only run into the barn to get out of the deluge of rain that had rolled over the ranch. She had not expected to see him. Her one obsession… *Chase*. Since he'd come to the Flying Kangaroo Ranch to train their champion racehorse Devil's Advocate, Sophia had been secretly watching Chase's every move.

Flicking her eyes to his face she could see his lopsided grin. He had caught her checking him out… and he seemed to relish the idea. His brilliant blue eyes sparkled with amusement and he flashed his gleaming white teeth at her.

A cool breeze wafted across her wet clothes. "I don't know what y… you…you're talking about, and really, shou…should…shouldn't you be wearing more clothes," she said from between chattering teeth, vigorously waving her hand up and down towards him.

Chase strode towards her, and in three large steps he was in front of her. His blue eyes darkened slightly as they flicked over her wet clothing, then shot back to her face. God he was so close, Sophia could feel the heat emanating from his body through her cold, wet clothes. A strong musky scent mixed with faint smell of horses and leather wafted over her.

He leaned in, and she took that moment to inhale his fragrance, causing her senses to spin slightly from the headiness of his scent. His warm breath fanned over her cheek and ear, "I'm not the only one who's a little under-dressed am I, Darling?" He ran his tongue slowly over the shell of her ear and moved his thumb backwards and forwards over her sensitive nipple.

Sophia whimpered slightly from the sensations shooting through her body, as her nipple acted like a puppeteer string to her clit. She moaned as Chase pinched her nipple and rolled it between his thumb and forefinger.

"So responsive darling," his lips moved across her cheek like a

Cocktails

scorching trail. "I think I'd love to see you with nipple rings," he murmured, pulling on both nipples simultaneously. Sophia cried out as the twin sensations shot through her body.

She felt his hands glide back down as the grabbed the base of her wet shirt. "Let's get you out of those wet clothes, and warmed up," he said, stripping her. He pressed his heated body closer, causing her to move back until she felt the wooden slats of the stall push up against her back. His hot mouth roaming down her neck as one large masculine hand cupped her breast. His warm mouth enveloped a nipple, then sucked slightly, his tongue teasing its tip. Sophia's whole body was burning.

Kneeling down, Chase made quick work of removing her jeans and boots. Feeling slightly self-conscious Sophia crossed her arms across her belly. She wasn't like the other girls he usually brought home, she was short and plump. Far from the svelte fitness models she mostly saw enter and exit his trailer.

He looked up at her through his mop of brown curls and gently drew her arms apart. "Don't cover yourself Sophia, you're beautiful." She flushed red. It was the first time he had used her name throughout this whole encounter. Sitting back on his feet he gazed at her momentarily, before he moved upward on his knees. He ran his hands up her outer thighs, to her breasts then back down to her waist. Leaning in, he kissed a blazing trail from the tip of each breast, down her waist, to the gentle swell of her stomach. "So beautiful," he murmured against her skin, "like satin and velvet."

Leaning back against the wooden planks Sophia groaned as her breasts swelled further and her body ached. She pressed herself outwards as she sought that scorching touch. "Move your legs apart, Darling." His voice was rougher and deeper than usual, she looked down and his blue eyes were darker, intent and staring up at her. Patiently, waiting for her compliance.

Sophia allowed him to move one of her legs on to his shoulder. Her swollen clit begging for him. She felt his warm tongue gently touch the swollen nub, then move backwards and forwards, gently before his lips encompassed and sucked on the little bud. The tension in her body heightened, and her breath quickened.

"More," she moaned, panting and gripping her fingers in his hair as

Cocktails

he worked his magical mouth over the swollen flesh. She tugged at him, trying to insist he move faster in his ministrations. Chase deliberately slowed down. "No," she cried out.

He stopped and looked at her. "You're impatient aren't you? " He grinned at her, then gently ran the index of his finger around her clit, whilst reaching up and tweaking a nipple. "I think a chain between your nipple and clit would be ideal," he said as he pinched her nipple and clit at the same time, "what do you think Sophia?"

Sophia cried out. *Oh God, the sensations, I can't handle them, I think I'm going to implode.* Her brain went into overdrive. "Yes, yes, anything, just give me what I need," she panted out.

He grinned up at her, then looked over at his stock saddle resting on the wooden saddle rack. Standing up, he moved his body into hers, a slight sheen of perspiration had begun to cover his muscular chest. "How badly do you need to come, Sophia? Will you do what I say?" He whispered, his breath feathering over her parted lips as his fingers moved between her swollen pussy, and a finger delved into her wetness. Sophia groaned again and fell against him.

"Anything?" she groaned, "I'll do anything."

Moving a finger inside her channel, his thumb brushed briefly over her swollen clit, as his lips claimed hers. His mouth plundering the sweetness as his tongue swept inside her mouth. *God this feels like heaven... and hell.* Sophia felt his finger moving in the rhythmic motion, driving her to almost madness as she could feel herself sliding to the edge. Suddenly he withdrew both his hand and mouth.

"No," she moaned.

Taking her hand Chase lead her to the saddle, she was too caught up in her bodies whirling responses to even worry when he had her lean over the saddle and he deftly tied her feet and hands to the wooden rack

"Very nice," she heard him murmur. A box was opened and he came back to stand in front of her with a gleaming bridle and a leather crop. "I bought these for you," he said softly, crouching down in front of her. Reaching out he ran a finger down her cheek gently.

"Do you trust me, Sophia?"

She looked at the equipment he held in his hands and looked into his beautiful blue eyes and nodded once. Chase seemed to let out a small sigh of relief.

Cocktails

"Open up sweetheart," he said rubbing his thumb over her bottom lip. "First I'm going to put that pretty mouth to use."

Within seconds Chase had removed his jeans and stood in front of her. His cock was standing huge, tall and proud. He gripped it at the base of his shaft. "You do this to me Sophia," he rasped, running his handed from shaft to base. Her eyes were wide from the sheer girth of it.

He placed the tip against her lips. Sophia ran her tongue over the weeping head, tasting his saltiness. "I want to fuck your pretty mouth, Sophia, I want to see my cock in your mouth." Sophia shuddered in anticipation and opened her mouth, allowing his cock to glide over her tongue and stretch her mouth, until it reached the back of her throat, causing her to gag slightly. He groaned audibly when she swallowed. Withdrawing, he then shuttled back in, over and over again. Sophia felt him grip her hair as he fucked her mouth. "So beautiful." Chase's voice was guttural. "I love seeing my cock going in and out of your pretty mouth."

Warmth spread throughout Sophia and she could feel her juices running down the inside of her legs from the excitement. She felt almost disappointed when he withdrew from her, replacing his cock with the rubber bit of the bridle. Fastening it to the back of her head he ensured it was secured tightly. "I hope its comfortable, Darling, "he whispered into her ear. "You're about to get the ride of your life."

Moving around behind her she felt him smooth a hand over her left buttocks before a sharp sting from the riding crop. "God so pretty," as he ran his hand over the mark soothing it, before swatting her again. She felt him press his warm lips to the stinging mark. Her body loved it. Every hit that he gave her. She was so close to orgasm, when she felt him move his long fingers down to her pussy.

"So wet, so ready," he inserted one finger, and pumped it in and out, before inserting two, then three. Stretching her, and causing Sophia to groan into the bit. Briefly he moved away causing her to whimper from the loss. Hearing the crinkling of a wrapper, she felt Chase grip onto her bridle once more, before pulling back and causing her neck to arch. He slammed his cock into her pussy, and she screamed from his invasion, causing her vaginal muscles to clench violently.

He pulled out and slammed back in, all the while keeping her head taut with the bridle. Chase pistoned into her over and over again, she could feel every huge inch of him as his cock slammed against her cervix. Sophia came with a scream, her inner muscles clenching, as he kept pumping until he wrenched a second orgasm from her. Her teeth biting down hard on the bit as she came. She felt it when he came as he shuddered and pulsed within her before he collapsed across her back, releasing the slack on the bridle he'd been gripping.

Panting heavily he gasped out, "Are you okay, Sophia?" Undoing the bridle so it fell from her mouth.

"Holy shit," she gasped, "You can ride me any day, Cowboy."

She heard him chuckle as he withdrew from her body, causing her to feel slightly bereft.

Untying her, he crouched down in front of her, his blue eyes gazing at her intently, "I think we will be doing this a lot more my beautiful Sophia," as he pressed his lips to hers, "because you are mine."

"As you are mine," she kissed him in return.

R.L. Phoenix *educates young minds in Science in a high school. She loves working with teenagers, helping them to meet their potential. She grew up in rural NSW on a farm, and the first vehicle she drove was a tractor. She has been a voracious reader since she was a small child, and has only recently taken up writing. She now calls Melbourne home, and has been inspired by its many writing networks.*

Red Lotus
— Samira Wyld

Kath stared at the baseball cap nestled amongst the books on the shelf. It was a reminder of what went before. A reminder of Andy. Long blonde hair, olive skin that was as smooth and ripe as any delicious young boy she'd met. His smell of sandalwood and cypress pine hung in the air. How long had it been, an hour, twenty minutes? Kath had lost track of time, the only time she remembered was with Andy. Inside her, pushing her knees toward her chest raising her to meet him, naturally finding the G spot the women's mags talked about. It did exist after all. At least it did, with Andy.

Something was amiss — something she couldn't put her finger on. Andy had left in a hurry, leaving his cap behind. At least he'd be back. This was something she was sure of because the two articles of clothing that mattered to him most were his cap and shoes. He once told her that he had an identity crisis if he didn't cover his hair.

It wasn't until she crawled from her sleepy sexed up sheets and headed for the kitchen did she think there was something in fact very wrong. Andy's shoes, Nikes, white with blue stripes sitting on the chair. Two shoes sitting side by side.

Waiting.

Waiting on the chair for Andy to pick up and put on. He'd place his shoes on the chair, side by side, loosening the laces with precision. His clean, long lean fingers pulling at them with certainty before he sat down to lace them one by one with vigour. His hair perfectly in place held by his cap. He'd glance up at Kath with his deep blue eyes with a 'Come fuck me look'. Kath didn't have a problem with that, for she always wanted him. Her groin ached at the thought. *Yes, he would definitely be back.* She padded barefoot around the kitchen and put the kettle on.

"Wait a minute," Kath mumbled. *Did he even leave? First his cap, now his shoes?* She mused over this as she methodically set about placing tea leaves of green and jasmine into the small aluminium pot, battered with age. She pulled a butcher's knife from the wooden rack and sliced up some mint from the jar on the window sill.

Cocktails

The reminder on her white board in bold large letters 'CALL WASTE DISPOSAL' glared at her. She'd forgotten to ring again! Annoyance teetered on the edge of her mind but she quickly dismissed it as she opened the fridge and reached for the milk. *Something on the floor.* A crumpled piece of paper.

Kath gripped the milk bottle to her chest, the corners of her mouth drew tight. Two shoes side by side, just sitting on the chair. She bent down crouching at the knees and the physical action of doing so caused her to hunger. A prickling desire that tingled deep in her belly, the warm afterglow of great sex and the desire to do it all over again.

Kath sat opposite the shoes to unravel the scrunched ball. She slowly prised it apart revealing the words within. Kath's hands turned as white as the paper she held, when she read the first line. She rubbed at her chest, and clawed at her throat, gasping for air. She stared at the shoes then kicked the chair with such force the shoes went flying. No longer neatly side by side, they now sat at deranged angles on the kitchen floor. The strong smell of Jasmine wafted in the air, and Kath knew full well, the tea had brewed too long.

By the time she read the second line, she slumped forward and squeezed herself as though she were in pain. The tears that followed stopped her from reading more. She dropped the crumpled note and headed into the bedroom.

She crawled beneath the sex-stained sheets that smelled of wet flour. She clung to Andy's scent of sandalwood and the fading smell of Jasmine tea. The letter had been short but not sweet. Andy's words cut her. Her wounds real or imagined lined the walls of the tiny apartment, closing in on her, threatening to smother her with more words of torment. She wrestled and grappled with what she had learned. Twisting, turning and hurting. The sheets wrapped around her leg and into her crotch, her nakedness wet with imagined blood as the wounds of his words cut deeper and deeper etching into her piece by piece.

Kath half fell out of bed in an attempt to untangle herself from the sheets, and ran to the bathroom. She looked at herself in the mirror — naked. Her perfectly rounded breasts, erect pink nipples, the sensual swell of her belly, and the perfect fine layer of black hair over her mon pubis, reminded her that she was indeed all woman. And then in a blink,

Cocktails

disgust crossed her face, as the vision of beauty faded. She grabbed the dressing gown from behind the door and wrapped it around her body tight, dispelling the image of flesh and breasts and rounded hips. More important things needed her attention. She had the matter of the shoes. But for now she was going to ignore everything, the letter, the shoes, the cap — Andy. All of it. She tipped the remains of the over brewed tea down the toilet and set about making a fresh pot while she hummed a tune.

A heavy breeze whipped at her face as she pushed the window open, the air becoming too oppressive from inside the flat. The shoes beckoned, as though calling her. She read the note again. It was a shopping list: bread; milk; tea...but she'd cleverly decoded it for what it really said: ugly; oversexed; I don't love you anymore. She squeezed it tight into her fist and her face flushed hot. She grabbed Andy's cap and threw it out the open window. She picked one of the shoes up off the floor and rummaged in the top drawer of her dresser for the pinking shears. She cut the laces until there was nothing left, and then tore up the shoe until all that remained was shattered pieces of cloth, and vinyl, and leather in her lap.

Kath took off her dressing gown and wrapped the remains of the mutilated shoe inside the folds, and headed for the back door. No time to dress, no time for modesty, no time to care. She found a shovel in the back shed and proceeded to dig and dig until the hole was equal measures wide and in length. Plenty large enough to conceal a flannelette dressing gown and a dismembered shoe. Before she covered it with dirt she retrieved the cap that had fallen amongst the rose bushes. She threw it in with the shoe concealing the existence of either.

Once inside her flat, Kath ran a hot bath scented with apricot oil. The remaining shoe she now placed on the edge of the bath. She placed one muddy foot after the other slowly into the bath. She washed Andy from her, every trace of scent gone as she brushed the back scratcher vigorously all over her body turning it pink. Kath stared at the shoe. The one remaining shoe. It was all she needed, it was enough of a reminder of who he was and how he made her feel.

She wrapped the large bath towel around her body, its abrasiveness from age and too many washes scratched at her already frazzled and

Cocktails

rejected body. She hung it on the door handle and pulled on a figure hugging red dress. The perfect kind of red. Rich and deep, its texture velvety like the red lotus, her favourite flower. She liked the way it wrapped around her curves. It was so tight, wearing underwear would've ruined the perfectness of the dress.

Back in the bedroom she ripped off the soiled sheets and rolled them over and over in her hands before throwing them in a black garbage bag. The bag she would later drop off at St Vinnie's. Sheets she no longer wanted. Their new owners could wash the stains of Andy from them, not her.

The door bell chimed. Kath glanced at the clock on the wall. Ten minutes early. She threw the doona without a cover over the mattress and yelled, "Just a minute."

She grabbed Andy's shoe from the bath, allowing her fingers to fondle the laces. The laces Andy once did up with such intensity. She climbed the small ladder inside her closet and pulled down the oversized hat box. She carefully opened the lid and looked at the other shoes inside. A black Doc Marten boot, a thong, the cheap Australian kind with the blue rubber strap, a white running shoe, a business shoe, just some among many and now Andy's shoe with the blue stripes. All a reminder of the men who once wore them. All distinct to their personalities and not all good lovers, in fact not many were at all. She felt deeply saddened by the loss of Andy. The note she had carefully decoded had cut her deeply. How dare he say those dreadful things about her?

"Such a waste," she whispered before sealing the lid. Kath placed it with great care back in the far corner of the walk-in-robe. She teetered on the ladder rung but found her footing in time. Smoothed down her dress and answered the door.

Peter kissed her hard, handing her flowers, and a bottle of expensive red wine. "What took you so long?"

"Shoes," Kath said. She took the flowers and the wine and put them on the kitchen bench.

Peter looked her up and down following her. "But you aren't wearing any."

"Exactly." She smiled.

Cocktails

He embraced her pushing her against the wall and kissed her passionately, tongue exploring her mouth meeting her own. He tasted sweet. His penis pressed hard against her thigh. She shook with desire and a guilty longing.

"I have no knickers on either," she whispered.

He groaned with pleasure and carried her into the bedroom, and lay her on the sheet less bed. As Peter entered her, she moaned in wanting, and for a moment thought about Andy. Her Andy, the perfect lover.

Peter pushed further inside her, and she raised her legs to meet his rising pelvis. He thrust hard. Again and again. Waves of orgasm finally rocked her. Thank God he knew how to satisfy her because the disposal was jammed so bad this time it could take at least a week to fix.

If Peter kept this up she could put up with him for a least that long.

Samira Wyld *is a Brisbane based writer, playwright and director. Her short fiction has appeared in several Australian and International anthologies. Samira is taking her Independent Theatre Company,* Wyldlake Productions *to Sydney in 2015 where she will be directing her latest play* The Audition. *Samira has backpacked extensively through third world and developing countries. She is passionate about travel and loves to draw upon these experiences to evoke a real sense of place in her storytelling.*

The Vibrator
— Derek Wayne

DING-DONG

Olivia worked her earring into place as she walked sprightly across her expansive living room. She had just returned from the courts and still wore her tennis-whites and headband.

DING-DONG

"I'm coming," she yelled, opening the door.

"Then perhaps I'm not needed." His smile was the first thing she saw, so megawatt brilliant it nearly blinded her. "I'm Jake, the vibrator repairman," he said, to relieve her obvious confusion.

"Oh, right, right. Come in, Jake, please."

"You have a lovely home," he said. He wore a snug, blue jumpsuit with the dildo-embossed logo of Johnson Sex Toys stenciled across the back. Olivia's eyes travelled downward to admire his backside.

"Thank you," she said. "And you have a nice, tight ass."

"I try to stay in shape." He tapped the toolkit in his hands. "So, having problems with your vibrator?"

"It's so frustrating." Olivia had placed her sexual aid on the foyer table earlier. She picked it up, handed it to Jake. "In certain positions it just shuts off, and I have to remove it and shake it to get it working again."

"Well, that won't do. Quite annoying, I'm sure."

Olivia took off her headband and the scrunchie that held her ponytail. She shook her shoulder-length blonde hair free. "It's the timing as much as anything. It's like the thing knows when I'm just about ready to come."

Jake laughed as he unscrewed the bottom of the eight-inch phallus. "I don't think this model has orgasm detection," he joked. He pulled a penlight from his kit and peered into the casing. "What you're describing sounds like a short, but I don't see anything obvious. Could you show me how you're using it when it shuts off?" He screwed the cap on and handed it back to her.

"Oh, sure," Olivia said. "Is the sofa in the den okay?"

"Wherever you're most comfortable."

Cocktails

Olivia slipped off her shoes, socks, and then her white skirt and panties. She slouched back on the sofa, spread her legs. "Sorry, I'm still a bit sweaty from my workout."

"No need to apologize. Your pussy looks incredible."

"I'll bet you say that to all your customers." Olivia turned on the vibrator and lightly rubbed it over her puffy sex lips. "I'm usually gentle at first, sort of playful. As I get more aroused, I work the tip in deeper." She tried to use the vibrator to part her lips, but she wasn't wet enough.

"Here," Jake said, reaching into the chest pocket of his jumpsuit. "I have some lubricant."

"Oh, perfect." She held the toy up, turned it as he squeezed out a liberal amount of lube. "Much better," she said, reinserting. And then she moaned. "Mmm... yes, much better."

"It seems to be working fine," he said, pulling at his collar, the room perhaps feeling a bit stuffy. "Are there any other ways you, ah... use it?"

Before she could answer, they were interrupted by the opening of the front door. Olivia's husband walked in. He took off his jacket and loosened his tie as he made his way to the den to put his briefcase down. He paused, seeing the younger man standing in front of his wife. A blink later, he noticed her spread legs and glistening cunt. "Hey, what's going on here?"

"Hi, Honey," Olivia said, not bothering to pause her masturbating. "This is Jake. Jake, this is my husband, Tucker." The men shook hands. "Jake is here to fix my vibrator. Remember I told you it keeps cutting off?"

"Oh, yeah. Women and their vibrators," he said to Jake, shaking his head. "But I don't have to tell you, huh?" Tucker bent over and gave his wife a quick kiss. "I'm grabbing a beer. Jake, you want anything?"

"Ice-water would be nice. Thanks."

"Olivia?"

"No, thanks. I'm fine."

Tucker left for the kitchen. Olivia and Jake turned their focus back on Olivia's problem. "So," she said. "Once I'm sufficiently aroused, I rub harder, like this. Then I'll push it into my cunt, just a few inches to start."

The vibrator continued to hum perfectly. "It's just like my car," Jake said. "It makes a noise every day for a month, until my mechanic listens

— then nothing."

"Exactly," she agreed. "Jake, do you mind if I take off my top? I'm getting awfully horny, and I enjoy playing with my nipples when I masturbate."

"I don't mind at all. Really, just pretend I'm not here."

Tucker returned with Jake's water and a beer for himself. "What a day," he said, plopping down beside Olivia. "I'm sorry. I don't mean to interrupt, but do either of you care if I jack-off? He added quickly, "I could go upstairs if it's a problem. I just hate to waste the... ah... visual." Tucker's eyes were glued to the vibrator as it probed deeper between his wife's legs.

"It won't bother me if it doesn't bother Jake," said Olivia.

"No problem here," the repairman said.

Tucker unzipped his pants and fished out his small cock. He flopped it around, trying to get hard. After a moment, Olivia recognized his difficulty and helped by bringing her foot up on the sofa, placing it on his crotch.

"Foot fetish," she said to Jake, as way of explanation. Tucker's cock rose quickly after that, and before long, he was stroking himself to match his wife's rhythm.

Then, as Olivia slid the vibrator to poke into her asshole, the toy suddenly shut off.

"There," she said, the dildo two inches deep in her butt. "This is what I was saying."

Jake knelt on the floor between her knees. "Okay, hold still, ma'am. I'm going to try to open the back without moving the vibrator." His hands replaced hers, but the machine shifted slightly in the exchange and cut back on. "All right. I'm going to move it around a bit and see if I can get it to quit again." He moved left and right, up and down, all the while inching slowly deeper into her asshole.

"Oh my, Jake. That's... ah, wonderful."

Tucker stood to get a better view, continuing to stroke himself.

Jake had pushed in several more inches when the vibrator cut off again. "There. Try to hold still." He left the plastic cock lodged a good six inches in her butt as he unscrewed the back. Again, he searched the inner mechanics with the help of his penlight. "Ah, I think I see the problem."

Cocktails

DING-DONG

"Come in!" Olivia and Tucker yelled together.

"Hello?" called a timid voice from the front door.

Olivia recognized their newest neighbor. "We're in the den, Stacy."

Stacy was a pixie-cut redhead with a gymnast's body and a mischievous smile. The jeans she wore hugged her taut ass like paint. She wasn't wearing a top. "Oh, I'm sorry. I didn't mean to interrupt." She smiled nervously at Tucker's erection.

"Nonsense," Olivia said, taking a long moment to admire Stacy's modest boobs. "It's actually a lot less formal than it looks. Jake, here, is trying to fix my finicky vibrator — AND MAKING ME HORNY AS HELL," she added, loud enough for Jake to hear from his position between her legs. "And Tucker just got home so, of course, he's jacking off."

Tucker smiled weakly, his eyes glued to Stacy's prominent pink nipples.

Stacy blushed. "Ah, well... I'll just come back another time."

"But you've already taken off your top, and..." Olivia hesitated as the situation became clear to her. "You thought I'd be in the shower after tennis and you came over to catch me before I got out. Right?"

A crimson flush washed over Stacy's face, spreading down her neck and ending at the top of her freckled tits. "It's just that you've been so nice to me since I moved in, what with the house-warming orgy you threw me, and all the porn you let me borrow. I just thought I'd come over and, ah... return the favour." Stacy's eyes drifted down to Olivia's swollen cunt.

"Oh, aren't you just the sweetest," Olivia said. "Well, there's no way you're leaving now with that image of your scrumptious little ... oh... oh my. I wasn't expecting that." Olivia's vibrator began to buzz again, only this time it was buried deep in her ass.

"Yeah," Jake said. "I found the problem — faulty relay. I replaced it, so you should be good to go." He got up from the floor and approached Stacy. "I was a little busy when you came in. I'm Jake," he said, extending his hand.

"Stacy." She took his hand, cupped it over her bare breast, and smiled. "Nice to meet you."

Jake lightly pinched her nipple, just to be social.

"Hey, I have a great idea," Tucker said, continuing to toss his cock

Cocktails

around in his hand. "Why don't you guys stay for supper? I'm making my legendary chilli."

"Oh... I don't know," Stacy said.

But Olivia wouldn't hear it. "That's a marvelous idea, Tuck. Come on, Stacy. We can have some pre-meal sex while Tucker cooks." Tucker's expression sagged. "Then we can have sex again for dessert," she added for her husband.

Stacy eyed Jake tentatively. "Well... I guess that would be okay."

"Great. Jake, are you in?"

Jake flashed his movie-star smile at both the girls. "Oh, I'd jump at the chance to be in either one of you." He began unzipping his jumpsuit.

"Then it's settled," Olivia said. "Tucker, how long will you be in the kitchen?"

"About half an hour," Tucker sulked. "But I was really hoping to... ah, you know... first."

Olivia shook her head. "Now don't be silly, Tuck. We both know how totally useless you are after you come." Still he pouted. "How about after we eat, you fuck me from behind while Stacy rubs her feet on your face?" Tucker gave a sideways smile. Olivia countered. "Okay... how about you fuck Stacy from behind while I rub MY feet in your face?" That suggestion brought out Tucker's horny grin.

Olivia's eyebrows rose to gain Stacy's approval. When Stacy smiled and nodded, Olivia said, "Looks like we have a plan."

Tucker padded off to the kitchen, leaving the others to their appetizer sex.

"You are so amazing," Stacy said to Olivia. "It's like you just know what everyone needs, even before they do."

"Oh, I don't claim to be God's own whore, or anything." Olivia casually took in Jake's tanned, muscular body. It didn't go unnoticed that his cock was nearly twice the size of her husband's. "I guess I'm just a people-person," she said, her cunt spread invitingly, the vibrator still purring quietly in her ass. "Now, about that favour you came to give me..."

"You want me to move the vibrator first?" Stacy asked.

Olivia smiled. "Only if you're planning to push it in deeper."

Cocktails

Derek Wayne *is a lucky husband, a proud father, and an unapologetic smartass. Fluent in sarcasm, and much less funny than he thinks he is, his life is filled with poignant whimsy. Derek's writing is inspired by a keen observation of the human condition and a naturally dirty mind. When not writing, he spends his time teaching our youth how to run fast and hit each other. Derek has previously been published in the Stringybark anthology,* Valentine's Day.

Harvey Wallbanger
— Meg Main

To wake up and find two tree snakes mating on the laundry ramp was disconcerting, but that's all. I was intrigued rather than disgusted. When a few days later one fell out of the exposed rafter and on to my bedside table sending jars and books crashing, it was hideous.
They had to go.
I phoned the man.
This is the moment to confess that I am now fifty-three, and after a lifetime of hearty sexual encounters both within and without wedlock, I have lately developed a strange aversion to men and sex. Perhaps this is because of the cancer. Having one boob half the size of the other removes all desire to flaunt. Perhaps it is a normal (albeit unacknowledged) state for women of my age. Most likely, as is well documented, I have become invisible and this reluctance is merely self defence.
I live alone, not even a cat, whose presence might have deterred the snakes.
The man, described in the local phone book as 'Harvey the Snake Catcher', duly arrived the next morning. He timed his arrival with the morning sunshine and maximum heat on the back of the house and the laundry ramp. That's where they had been most mornings, so far only two of them, but there was no telling. The one in the rafters had unnerved me badly.
"They bask then," he said.
"I know that," I countered. "And they mate then too."
Harvey grunted at that. I took him for a taciturn man. He was huge, not fat, just large in every way. He must have been about six foot, four inches tall. His torso was vast like an oak barrel I once saw in Germany and it sprouted all over with thick, black clumps of curly hair. They erupted around his vest armholes and under his arms and across his back and above the neckline of the blue singlet. All this robust hirsuteness contrasted incongruously with his utterly bald and shining pink head. In one ear lobe he wore a gold stud and in the other, a gold ring. Tattoos

Cocktails

down both arms completed the riveting picture.

I couldn't take my eyes off him. He had an interesting mouth, not smiley but sensitive, I thought, and wide.

He refused the obligatory offer of a cup of tea or coffee in favour of a glass of water, and then pulling on a pair of gloves as he walked down the hallway to the laundry, he turned to me, "Quiet now," he said. Me! Quiet! I weigh fifty kilograms and was tiptoeing behind, noting his scuffed boots the size of my snorkelling flippers, and simultaneously, how quiet he was in them. He glided.

Typically the snakes were nowhere to be seen despite the hot sun. Harvey squatted down to peer into the vent between the bricks from whence they had previously emerged and as he did so, his jeans pulled down slightly, straining over his muscular gluteals, and there was another tattoo, nestled amongst dark tufts, leading down invitingly. What was the image? I bent closer over his bent back, squinting in the bright sunshine and inhaling deeply his fresh sweat smell. It looked like two mating snakes, one red and one yellow, disappearing south into the dark.

He stood up abruptly nearly knocking me off the ramp. Then he stood on my toe. There was a moment's embarrassed confusion as I tried to explain that I too had been bending over, above him, trying to see into the same hole. "You could have looked from the other side," he said. "You would have had a better view." He gave me a thoughtful look. Then he said, "They appear to be living in this wall cavity. It's quite a common place for them to choose: warm and dry. Comfy." He gave the brick wall above a sharp bang with his fist. "Just call me Harvey the Wall Banger," he laughed. I smiled but it was forced through unreasonable disappointment. It sounded like an old joke

"Now what?" I asked hopefully, looking straight ahead at a large blue-inked eagle rising gloriously up out of the material of his singlet just above nipple level. I daren't look at his face, my own still burning from the bending incident.

"Well, if they won't come out then I can't catch them." I thought that was stating the obvious but nodded encouragingly. "However, (I liked that word coming from him) I have come prepared." He smiled, "I have two funnel traps in my car. I'll show you how to set them up and what

Cocktails

to do once you've got a snake in one of them."

"I'll call you."

"Absolutely no need. You'll be fine. Just take them down over the other side of the creek and release them there. They shouldn't come back."

He demonstrated. First the funnel traps, then the big black bag into which the traps are inserted and finally how to seal the big back bag by flicking it round with little golf club-like implements. I didn't take too much notice, though I tried. His voice, his mouth, the black hairs on the backs of his surprisingly delicate hands — I just couldn't concentrate.

I would definitely call him I decided, as soon as one of them was in the trap.

This time he said, "yes" to the coffee offer. Then, "On second thoughts, any chance of a beer? Make it my favourite brand and I'll drop twenty percent on your bill."

"Beer?" I checked the clock. He noticed.

"The sun is well over the yardarm," he said.

Oh God. How impressive.

I did have beer, three cans, but the wrong brand it turned out.

"Ten percent off?" I asked. This was flirting, I think. I'd forgotten.

"Of course his fingers brushed mine as he took the glass. Of course they were wet, as were mine, from the condensation.

His eyes were deep brown, my favourite colour.

We talked snakes of course: types and lengths? Where and when? Had he ever been bitten and what then? He wasn't that easy to draw out about the snakes. He talked about the government. His views were not mine but no disappointment this time. Lunch time came around and beer was swapped for white wine, with a toasted cheese sandwich. With each sip of wine he seemed to touch me more. He touched my arm when he made a point. He touched my cheek when I laughed. At one point he reached over and moved a strand of my fringe aside.

I knew why was he still here? He was forty years old. I had established that. My mind behind my smiley face was in turmoil. Again? Could this really be happening again? When had I last showered? Would it be strange if I went and had one now? How clean were the sheets on the bed? What knickers did I have on? What about

Cocktails

the boob? Why had I ever stopped shaving my legs? Was he married? Of course I hadn't asked that. He wore no ring. My single state was pathetically obvious.

It began. He put his hand over mine as I reached to take his empty plate.

"The thing about mating snakes… " he said softly.

"Yes I know." Me, helpless before this bald and wily charmer.

Still sitting down he reached for my other hand. Warm fingers, short dirty nails. I was looking down towards our linked hands. All I could see was the rising in his trousers.

"Why don't we take off our clothes and lie in the sun?" he suggested.

I couldn't think of one good reason not to. "Like the snakes," I offered inanely. Then I said, "But the wood will be too hard."

"Spread a blanket."

"I… I… my breast. I've had surgery," I stuttered.

Deliberately, slowly, he released his right hand and still holding my left, he undid the top three buttons of my blouse. Of course there was no bra. I didn't dare look down but he did. Eyes wide open he looked long and hard. Then he bent his enormous, glistening head and so gently, so exquisitely, he kissed the puckered nipple.

I was lost, aching with the sort of desire not felt since I was sixteen, the sort that lodges between the thighs and can only be assuaged by one thing. I would have lain down on the bare boards at that point, in full view of all the neighbours if need be.

Harvey released my other hand and peeled off his vest. More curly black hair and blue tattoos than I could bear. I dropped my eyes back to the bulge. He undid my last few buttons. I began to shake. Boots off. Trousers and underpants yanked off in one impatient tug. I was pulling at my own shorts, desperate to be rid of them, feeling the surprising sun, his even more surprising looking, at my skin — everywhere.

The huge rearing of it, amongst its black nest. I knelt to lie down.

"Blanket!" he reminded.

I grabbed the throw off the couch, threw it over the hot boards and naked, we both dived for it. I, who have always valued foreplay almost more than the act itself, couldn't get him in fast enough. The pulsing need was consuming me. No tongues, no fingers. Just this. The urgency

Cocktails

was such that I came almost immediately, a premature ejaculation, if you will; a gaping, vast, primal contraction pulling him in deeper and deeper. He waited. Then he waited some more; long, slow thrusts igniting and releasing me again and again.

Later I turned him over and ran my tongue over his cavorting snakes as I'd wanted to since the morning.

And again.

Until finally two sated, sun-soaked snakes lay spent.

Meg Main has recently alighted in Murwillumbah, northern NSW, after many years of living in Queensland and wandering in far flung places. She now spends most of her life in her car driving between family in Lismore and friends in Brisbane. But this gives plenty of thinking time. Murwillumbah is fecund. Gardening has become a necessity and may yet become a hobby. Another new found and time consuming interest is dragon boating. Meg writes compulsively, mostly odd notes and scribbles on bits of paper which get lost. Occasionally though, they coalesce into a short story. Meg has previously been published in the Stringybark anthology, Between Heaven and Hell.

Dusty Rose
— Shane von Liger

She had quit school, and sometimes she felt like she wanted to quit everything. The mornings were the worst. Like this one. She could have kicked the vacuum cleaner that she pushed around the lounge room, in the clunking circuit her boredom had carried her into, the mechanism sucking, like her life. She did kick it. She shoved it away. Filling carrier bags with grubby washing, she wondered how bored she could possibly get.

Ten heavy minutes later – no, *eleven*, fuck it – she lugged her bags into the laundrette. She fumbled with her purse. She had notes, but not the right coins. She sighed, and waited. Where was the fucking attendant? The plastic chair felt so hard and uncomfortable under her buttocks. It was barely wide enough. She remembered the feel of Eddie's hands, how he used to grip her cheeks and grind her down onto him when he was about to finish. It made her finish too, when he did that. Until she had found out about him fucking that anorexic little private school bitch. She had quit school, mainly, so she wouldn't have to see him. Not that she told anyone that.

She watched the machines spinning round and round with washing that belonged to other people. She looked out the window. Someone was standing at the bus stop outside. It was her neighbour, the pretty one. The bus pulled up at the stop. The wheels on the bus go round and round, she sang silently. Her neighbour got on the bus and sat down and didn't look at her. The wheels on the bus go fuck you. The bus pulled away. She would have her licence in a few months anyway. She planned to get a job delivering pizza. It was a way to meet guys and find out where they lived even before the first date.

The door swept open with a loud click. A guy walked in. She didn't think hot guys came to laundrettes. She took a breath.

They got talking over small change. Small change, small talk – but that was all it took. She felt the plastic in her hand replaced by gold. She wasn't looking anywhere but the deep greyness of his eyes. She couldn't think of things to say, but she said them anyway. She thought he would go. He was pulling things out of the dryer into the stuffy

Cocktails

overheated air. She saw the satin flash of crimson boxer shorts. His basket was nearly full. She began to prepare herself to feel sad, to load the machine alone, to wait a bit longer and then trudge home with her bundle of soggy washing. He astonished her with his bouquet of words.

"Do you want to come around and see my dust collection?"

A *dust* collection? Most guys would suggest coffee, or something alcoholic, or to watch TV. It wasn't normal, but what the hell.

"Sure." The main thing was that he had asked her. She gave him a look. It was a look she had practised, tilting her chin down, opening her lips just a little bit. The look said, here I am, a sweet shy girl next door, a warm, cuddly girl with a pussy made of magic.

She put her bags on the back seat of his car, his basket next to them. She liked the back seat. They drove around a long corner. He parked next to a tree on the nature strip, flower blossoms bursting over them in a lovely spray of pink droplets. They went inside, her footsteps soft in thick carpet pile. In the dim quiet of his small unit, she smelled his sweat, fresh and enticing. He opened the door to another room.

The dust collection was exactly that. Clean glass jars, on a shelf, stuffed with matted grey clumped in dense vertical cylinders, labelled with dates. They went back for years. She thought of particles of air that had died and drifted down, accumulating, piled and piled upon each other.

Her eyes wandered off the shelf. Through another doorway she could see a washing machine. She knew he knew which way she was looking. She had felt the air tense and quiver. She had to ask.

"Are you thinking what I'm thinking?"

"I think so."

In tandem they were at the car. They grabbed a bag each. The washing machine took all she had. As it started up they stepped back. They watched it. His arms went around her, fitting her body to his.

"*We are the dust of long dead stars.*" His whispered poetry touched her ears, caressed her hair. She turned around within his embrace.

It was a long, luscious kiss. She gave him more. She offered her mouth to his, to the force of his lips, their powerful suction. A force equally powerful was pulling at her clothing, lifting the garments from her body, dumping them on the floor. All of them. She undid his belt. She could feel his hard-on straining under his jeans. She opened the zip

Cocktails

and his cock sprang out, a long one, stretching its covered head towards her. He pulled her closer. His body pressed up to her, pressing her into the washing machine. His hand reached down, uncovered the head. She felt that long, straight cock slide inside her. She leaned into his breaths, into the building rhythm. She let it all happen. A deep shuddering began, her joy surging between man and machine, man and machine, man and man and man and man and man and *man* and *man!* and MAN and *MAN* and *MAN!* and . . . machine.

He wasn't done, but her back felt sore, her thighs too. They went to the bedroom. She climbed onto the bed while he hurried out of his jeans. She lay back in sweet comfort on the doona. She lifted her knees and then he was kneeling in between them, positioning, thrusting into her again. She felt the rhythm quickening. He pulled out. He leaned back, his cock filling his hand. She sat up and grabbed it. He closed his eyes.

She loved to play with penises, rubbing and squeezing the hard rubbery length of them; the way they swelled and throbbed and shot their stuff through the air. Some of his went onto the carpet. She found a tissue and reached out to clean it up. He stretched his arm around her and told her to leave it. He rubbed it into the carpet with his foot. The sticky wet smear glistened in the pile like a melting pearl.

"That'll be dust too before long," he said.

He settled down into the bed and pulled the covers over them. She nestled back into him. Her senses drifted in the warm happy fullness she always felt after a good fuck. She felt something else, too — a new tranquillity, a deep comfort in thinking that dust could soak up every little liquid clot life could throw at it.

The cylinders of dust, across the room, hovered into her vision. They could have been alien spacecraft newly landed on the shelves. She felt her eyes drawn towards them. She noticed the different colours first. She saw the greys of pale distant clouds, static on old TV screens, trapped dead mice, familiar footpaths. The clumps layered up, shading into each other. She began to see shapes in the grey — too vague to say what they were. Her eyes searched, more deliberate, more watchful. There had to be patterns. She wanted to find them.

She was about to give up and leave the dust to itself when she found one. A flower — made of dust, surrounded by dust. She saw the blurred outlines of the petals spreading open.

"Look," she said. She pointed and he looked. "A rose."

His arms drew her closer. He kissed her neck. "What we see is what we are," he murmured. "My dusty rose."

His hand slid down across her thigh, into her thicket of hair. She felt his fingers teasing through it. She knew how soon she could be ready again. His hand moved lower. He began to murmur something else. More poetry. It sounded familiar. The memory of the words drifted back to her from one of her school classes. His finger was inside her now. She didn't try to follow the words, but he spoke them in a rhythm, and the rhythm followed the shocks of pleasure his hand gave her. He was rubbing her the way she liked it — firm and steady and right on the spot. She felt her moisture welling up, seeping out. She caught a few words, the end of what he said: "*...this quintessence of dust.*" She had no idea what a quintest was, but the way he said it made her feel like the two of them were something special, something ultimate. She put her hand on his and rubbed herself with him, quicker and harder, until her whole body quivered and shook and left her gasping for breath.

He had driven her home, and kissed her. He had asked her for her number but they couldn't find a pen. She had stepped out of the car. She had gone around to the back window and with her finger written her number in the dusty glass. Then she had gone to the driver's side and kissed him again.

In the backyard she opened the bags under the washing line. She hung it all out. Then she leaped up, her feet launching her, her hands grabbing the rail, so light, so easy. She swung on the washing line. She spun, the wet fabrics bright around her, spinning with them, spinning and spinning.

Shane von Liger used to stay up late at night waiting for the Muse to visit him, but she would only ever send her uptight PA with an occasional bag of stale doughnut holes. One night her PA was off sick, so she sent Borat instead, who said to him, "Maybe we can follow her and make a sexy time with her." He has been doing this ever since.

The Buzzer
— Bernadette Frances

Her palms were sweaty.

She raised her glass, smiling out at the mostly uniformed crowd as she initiated the toast. Her eyes searched for those she was most desperate to have on her, and found that they were probably the only set that weren't.

Not even the applause that swirled around her could dull the disappointment she felt as she walked carefully from the stage. Her *Aide-de-camp* relieved her of the black folder she had clutched to her side as she returned to take her seat next to the shy wife of her one of her colleagues.

She wanted to take it all back… everything she had said to him, everything they had agreed to. She wound and then unfurled one long fingered hand from the stem of her glass, before she let it hover beside it, exposed to the cool air.

He still did not look at her.

She shifted slightly, her gaze skimming across the wrists of the uniformed officers and their wives with whom she was seated. None of their watches were visible.

Her smile wavered as her still damp hand returned to her glass. Tilting her head to one side, she politely nodded in response to her neighbour's nervously spoken comment about the food that had been placed before them.

The woman to whom she spoke didn't wear a watch either, nor, strangely to her thinking, did her husband who was seated to the woman's left.

Her little finger lifted from the table and led the others in a cascaded tap against it — an action she repeated several times before moving her hand, beneath the table, to the outside of her leg. She briefly felt the stiff cotton and synthetic mix of her uniform's long skirt, before her fingers found and traced the red ribbon that ran down the side of her thigh.

She was just flattening her damp hand against her leg when it was engulfed in another's.

Cocktails

Her relief was immediate. She looked at him as he returned her hand to the table and left it there, between their two place settings. The pads of his fingers rubbed over the top of hers in a gentle repetitive rhythm.

Her eyes moved to their joined hands, before lifting to look at his face. She smiled as she watched the edges of his green eyes crinkle as he turned to grin at her while he maintained his conversation with her boss, seated on his left. His other arm reached forward on the table, just enough so he was sure that she could see the white strip around his wrist where his watch should be.

He could do it at any time.

Her eyes squeezed shut as she took a deep breath in. The inevitability was both thrilling and frightening. She opened and turned her pleading eyes to him, but he had turned back to his conversation, his hand falling flat against the top of hers, the soft underskin of his wrist against hers. His fingers fell either side of her palm, squeezing gently but forcefully.

To cover the impulse to bite her lip, she lifted her glass to her mouth and drew the cocktail in between suddenly dry lips. She didn't return it to the table, instead she rested the glass's cool lip beneath hers, pausing, before taking another sip of the fizzy mix.

She licked her lips and murmured first, "Hmm." As she did so, and then "Yes…," the latter in unison with several others, also responding to another of her neighbour's comments.

Her goat's cheese tart lay untouched on her plate as she struggled to tame the anxiousness that was rooted in her stomach and chest, but whose tendrils had lodged themselves firmly in her throat. She watched the white gap on her husband's wrist now partially obscured by the cuffs peaking from within the cylinder of the arm of his grey dinner jacket.

She should never have agreed to do this.

She shifted in her seat, trying to sit in such a way as to alleviate her discomfort, knowing, even as she did so that it wouldn't help. Instead she was confronted with an increased awareness of just how far gone she was.

He removed his hand from where it had laid on top of hers and leant in towards her.

Her glass froze beneath her lips. Her breath stopped and she held perfectly, unnaturally still.

She felt him whisper against her temple. "Eat, Baby." His gentle lips

Cocktails

rested just long enough against her pulsing temple to allow him to reach down into her handbag.

Was it time? She thought as she watched him retrieve something from within the oversize clutch. She watched his hand as it re-emerged, tilting her head, her desperate eyes looking…

She saw only his olive skinned face, with its gently emerging beard.

Hope and dread duelled in her head, swirling in her chest and moved down her body tightening in her stomach. Her wanting now building in intensity to become need, making her clench inside.

His hand returned to lie atop hers while he spoke to the waitress who had appeared between them to fill his glass. She had no idea what he had said, but knew exactly what he now had in his pocket. She squeezed her legs together.

Even in the face of the possible humiliation that clamoured alongside her need, she knew there was no going back. She wondered how her junior officers and colleagues must be looking at them and what they may be seeing. Defensively, anger edged its way into her mind and she jerked her glass from her mouth and put it back on the table. What would they say? Not to her — they wouldn't dare. But what would they whisper about her to each other?

And suddenly she was on the verge of tears.

"Mel," he said, as though reading her thoughts, and all her fear, her anger and the 'what ifs' gave way at the quiet warning in his tone. Desperate need returned.

"Eat it," he mouthed, as his eyes moved from her to her untouched plate.

She picked up her cutlery and slipped her knife into the buttery pastry, cutting it in half. Methodically she halved the half, then the quarter, then the eighth. Playing — with no real intention to eat it, she speared a cheery tomato. Its skin burst apart, sending its seedy juice spurting up, off the plate to land on his jacket.

"Oh…," she gasped.

He looked at her.

"Mitch …I…"

Her voice was barely audible and tapered off as she shifted in her seat, her eyes following his finger as it moved along the material of his

Cocktails

jacket, scooping up the seeds. He watched her watching him as he put his finger into his mouth. She knew how his tongue would feel on his skin as he licked and swallowed.

She too swallowed. Her lips parted, her breathing quickened.

"Hmm." She heard him murmur as his other hand moved beneath the table. Her loudly beating pulse blocked out all other sound.

He indelicately gripped her long skirt and pulled it bunch by bunch upwards, exposing her stockinged legs. His hand slid beneath her skirt to hold its hem and push it slowly further up her leg towards her clenching crotch.

Her panicked wanting eyes were fixed on her plate. Her breathing quietly haggard as his hand approached the one place she knew he controlled tonight. The awareness of where they were, who she was and the promise of his actions bombard her, confusing her. Want and need.

He continued to talk with her boss as his hands moved gathered and moved more of the material up her leg, finding her suspenders.

She heard his gently uttered "Good girl." At which she looked briefly, indirectly at her neighbour dreading whilst also hoping that she had heard him too, but her attention remained elsewhere.

Desperately she tried to slow her breathing, fighting to control any outward sign of exactly where her husband's hand was and where she so desperately wanted it to be.

Breath in, 1, breath out, breath in, 2, breath out, breath in, 3, breath out… But his fingers had reached the juncture of her thighs and began to tap in the same cadence against her sensible cotton-covered pubis.

She carefully rested her knife on the plate and reached again for the wine glass, though it did not make it to her mouth. It instead became the sole occupant of her gaze, as she tried to remember the ingredients of a buzzer; orange juice, whiskey… champagne...

His tapping and her breathing met and danced in perfect unison. She was transported to a place of such intimacy, lost in a rhythm so private, so familiar that she forgot that she was anyone else other than his wife, his lover, his woman.

"Mitch…" escaped from between her barely open lips.

Her bosses' laughter covered the slap of her husband's hand on the bare skin above her garter. She started in the chair, very nearly dropping her glass.

Cocktails

Even as he spoke again to her laughing boss, his palm rubbed against her leg, before his fingers pressed one at a time against her now heating and she knew without seeing, reddened skin.

Her legs parted, her bottom slipped down slightly in the chair as she waited, breath baited, hoping... her internal clenching, becoming external, moving her to rock almost imperceptibly in her seat.

He slipped his hand down her leg, taking her skirt's hem with him, drawing it back over her knees leaving it to fall about her legs. As her gentle rocking continued she whispered so quietly, she was sure that he hadn't heard her. "Please..."

His hand moved away from her leg to sit curved against her neck, his palm against her skin, his fingers in her dark hair, his thumb resting along the curve of fair skin that moved to towards her chin.

The rocking of her hips increased in intensity. Her eyes looked straight ahead watching her Staff Officer and his animated wife across the room. She didn't care who saw anymore.

His fingers curved to move slowly up and down, into her hair, rubbing painfully yet gently against the taunt strands, loosening some them from the bun they were drawn tightly into.

She closed her eyes, savouring him, this. Them.

She didn't see his other hand as it reached into his pocket.

But she knew when he had reached it.

She didn't need to know the time anymore.

His eyes found hers as they opened, and he smiled as she did, her breath falling contentedly, relieved out of her as she felt the gentle buzz of the remote control vibrator fill her.

The time was now.

Bernadette Frances *is a Canberra based writer. An avid reader with a vivid imagination, Bernadette is never without a notebook and is forever wondering about the lives, silent or other, of those she observes. In an effort to counter a temporary case of writer's block, in August she took what was supposed to be a break from penning her novel to write her first short story and has not stopped since.*

Adios Motherfucker
— Michelle Irwin

Celeste's head pounded in time with the music as she appraised the dance floor. Her friend, Tia, had dragged her to the nightclub — which seemed filled to the brim with children — in a bid to put her divorce behind her, but the people around her only served to make her feel old and bitter. She turned to find Tia, but she'd disappeared.

"Great," Celeste muttered. "She's ditched me too."

"What?" A young man dancing nearby cupped his ear. There was something familiar about his brown, spiked hair and baby blue eyes, but she didn't know guys who wore eyeliner.

"I wasn't talking to you!"

"Huh?"

"Never mind!"

At the bar, a mob had lined up, pushing and shoving for their drinks.

"Have you had a wet pussy?"

Celeste spun in response to the voice. "Excuse me?"

The man from the dance-floor held up two pink shots. "Have you had a wet pussy?"

When she didn't answer, he stepped forward.

"Am I the first to give you a wet pussy?"

Is someone having a joke at my expense? "Do you have to keep saying that word?"

"What word?" He leaned in and brushed his lips against her ear. "Pussy?"

He offered her a glass. "Try it."

Celeste was about to refuse when she spotted Tia at the end of the bar giving two thumbs up.

"Bottoms up."

Celeste tipped her drink back. "What was that?"

"I told you, a wet pussy."

She blushed and the room grew hot.

"Was it worth the wait?" He was obviously aware of the effect he'd had on her.

Cocktails

Two can play at that game. "I've had better."

He narrowed his eyes, raised one finger and disappeared into the crowd. Before Celeste had time to consider what was happening, he'd returned with two cocktails.

"What's this?"

"The only thing that can follow a wet pussy." His gaze was scorching. "A screaming orgasm."

"I've never had one of those either. Will you give me my first?"

He held out a glass, but instead of taking it, she ducked her head and wrapped her tongue around the straw. With perfect eye contact, she drank deeply. His Adam's apple bobbed and his gaze left hers to focus on her mouth.

An instant later, the drinks were on a table, his lips were against hers, and his hands were in her hair. His breathing was heavy as his tongue brushed her lips. When her mind caught up, she pulled away.

"What's wrong?"

"I — I don't even know your name."

"Adam, it's Adam." He pressed his lips against hers again.

Despite the intensity of his kiss, she pulled away once more. "I don't think —"

Adam's kiss cut her off. "Don't think," he murmured, trailing kisses along her neck. Feather-light, his lips brushed over her skin.

"Why me?"

Adam stopped cold. "Are you kidding? You're the sexiest girl here."

"I'm hardly a *girl*."

"I beg to differ."

"What I mean —" She tried to stay focused on her argument as he trailed his fingers back and forth over her skirt.

"There are so many younger — Oh god!" His hand slipped underneath her hem.

His fingertip brushed across the front of her panties. "I don't want younger."

"I don't do the whole one night stand thing."

"Who said I do?"

"But —"

"Let's just see where this takes us."

Cocktails

Adam's fingers slipped beneath her panties and slid across sensitive flesh.

"Fuck it," she said. Almost breathless with need, she begged Adam to take her home. He wrapped his hand around hers and they rushed from the club.

Adam pressed a button on his keys and his garage door slid open. Celeste reached for his shirt and pulled his body against hers. The momentum slammed them both against the garage wall.

"Stop." His voice was quiet as he extracted himself from her hold. "I have to confess before we go on. I should've told you before, but I ... I thought you'd recognize me."

Still leaning against his garage wall, she froze.

"I know you. I —" he gave a nervous chuckle "—I've admired you for months."

Her mouth went dry at his admission.

"My brother and I have been regulars at your office recently."

She frowned as she tried to recall any regular visitors to the accounting firm where she worked. Brothers ... starting up a trendy ... *Oh, god!* "That's your club?"

"I hoped you'd realise."

"I can't be fraternizing with a client."

"Then don't. Call it a one-night stand with a stranger."

"That's worse." She ducked her head as the heat of the moment left her.

Adam guided her face to meet his gaze. "If you want to leave, I won't stop you. I'll drive you home, but I've wanted this for months."

"I don't know if I'm ready for this."

"I'm not asking you for undying love." He kissed her cheek.

Her body made the decision for her when her hands clutched at his hair as his kiss lingered before trailing to her jaw. She twisted and captured his mouth in a desperate caress.

Breathless with desire when they broke apart again, his impish smile lit his face.

"Should I be insulted you didn't recognise me?"

"You're usually more serious," she said, indicating his spiked hair and smudged make-up.

Cocktails

"You don't think I'm serious now?" he asked, looking at her through his lashes with a gaze so scorching that it practically burned her skin. She couldn't respond, she was pinned in his gaze.
"I am deadly serious." He claimed her lips again.

A trail of clothes followed their twisting path toward his bedroom. By the time they arrived, they were both in their underwear. Adam wrapped his arms around her and she sank into his welcome embrace. He kissed her collarbone, nudging her bra strap off her shoulder.
"You are so beautiful." His warm breath carried the words over her skin.
She slid her fingernails down his back as he pushed her bra out of the way and cupped her breasts. He rolled her nipples between his fingers and pressed open-mouthed kisses against her throat.
He sat back and watched as her ravenous need made her body quiver with anticipation. Once more, his gaze blazed trailed over her skin, as if he could barely believe she was in front of him. Then he pushed forward and crashed his lips to hers. With needful desperation, his tongue caressed and explored. His fingers tangled in her hair before dancing down her back to unclasp her bra. He peeled the black lace away from her skin and tossed it aside. His lips left her mouth and trailed the column of her throat.
Celeste threaded her fingers into his hair as she tipped her head to enjoy the feeling of his warm breath whispering adorations over her skin. Her fingertips scratched across his scalp as he moved down her body. With a soft kiss to the underside of her breasts, he trailed kisses across her stomach.
Kneeling before her, Adam paused for approval. Empowered by his attention, she nodded. With no more delay, he dragged her panties down her legs.
He sat back on his heels and his gaze followed the curves of her body. Their eyes met as he leaned in and pressed a kiss between her legs. She toppled backward as the shock of his mouth on her sent a spasm through her body. His fingers dragged along the sensitive skin on her thighs before he traced them over the soft flesh at her entrance. Celeste shifted her hips to let him know she was ready and then he pressed two fingers inside while his tongue traced circles over her sensitive skin.

Cocktails

It had been so long since she'd felt another's touch that she was pushed towards blissful oblivion faster than she'd envisioned. Her world was about to explode when he stopped. He moved away and she practically growled at him to keep going.

With a chuckle, he moved toward his bedside table, pulled out a foil pack and ripped it open.

"Let's see if you were paying attention earlier. First, there was the wet pussy. Then there was . . ." He pushed his boxers down while he waited for her to finish his sentence.

Celeste was beyond answering as she caught sight of his abs forming an arrow that pointed straight to his prominent erection.

She resisted shouting, "Gimme!"

Just.

He rolled the condom down his length, stroking it as her eager gaze took in every movement. He stalked toward her and she scuttled backward to make room. He was intimidating, but in a fantastic way.

"What comes after a wet pussy, Celeste?"

"A screaming orgasm?"

"Exactly," he said as he pushed himself deep inside her.

She tipped her head back as he moved with an excruciating, deliberate slowness. She could feel every inch of him as he moved all the way out and then rushed back in.

He rested one arm beside her head and used the other to trace patterns across her skin as their mouths melted together. His slow thrusts continued as he trailed his hand down her stomach. He circled his fingers across her clit, his touch spiralling her toward pleasure.

Again, Adam stopped right before she was able to find release. He sat up and guided her over him. Using a steady grip on her hips, he moved her to his own rhythm.

So close to the edge, her breath came faster and sounds escaped her that she'd never made before. Sex with her ex-husband hadn't been bad, but it had never been vocal. Now, she couldn't help herself.

His lips caressed her nipples in turn, and then he nipped at her sensitive skin. When he slipped his hand between them and grazed her clit again, there was no build-up. She saw stars and a primal cry tore from her throat.

Cocktails

At the noise, Adam moved faster, making her ride him as the waves of her bliss crashed over her again and again.

"I'm not finished with you yet," he murmured as he kissed her neck and guided her onto her back. It was clear his intent was to fulfil his own need, but the change in tempo sped her toward another release. Just as he stilled over her, she cried out again.

Celeste knew that whatever happened next, the ghost of her ex had been well and truly exorcised.

Adios, Motherfucker, she thought as she pulled Adam into a passionate kiss.

Michelle Irwin *lives in sunny Queensland in the land down under with her surprisingly patient husband and ever-intriguing daughter, carving out precious moments of writing and reading time around her accounts-based day job. A lover of love and overcoming the odds, she primarily writes paranormal and fantasy romance.*

Snow Ball
— Jim Baker

The light from a glorious full moon made the snow glisten, and the freezing cold air gripped us savagely as we left the relative warmth of our tent. All was still and silent. The Sherpas came out with hot tea and blessings, and then the two of us turned away from the campsite to begin our lonely trudge to the summit… and glory.

All went well at first, and then the weather deteriorated, as often happens on Everest. Soon we were battling a raging snowstorm that limited vision to no more than a few meters. We fought on, roped together, still in radio contact. Every step was a huge physical effort.

At 100 meters from the summit, Roger's voice rasped in my ears. "It's no good, Jim, I can't do any more." The rope tightened and I looked back to where I could just pick out his form, lying in the snow.

"Leave me. At least you might make it."

I hesitated for a moment, and then cut the rope. The snow was already forming his tomb. I battled on upward into the howling blizzard.

The last few steps were agony, but at last I reached the small plateau on the summit. Thick snow was still falling, but just as suddenly as it had sprung up, the wind abated. My oxygen was almost gone, I was totally exhausted, but nothing could take away the huge sense of achievement. I had climbed Everest, and I was standing alone on the top of the world…

… "Cocktail, sir?"

The voice shook me from my reverie and I whirled around. A small man, clad in a black tuxedo and sporting a black bow tie stood on the edge of the plateau. He walked over and proffered a silver tray on which rested a crystal glass, half full of yellow liquid. I stretched out a hand mechanically, picked it up, and sipped. The taste of advocaat, tinged with cognac, touched my lips. I took a larger sip, rolled the smooth liquor around my mouth, and swallowed. Blissful warmth spread through my body and I gave a sigh of pleasure.

"Highballs Ltd at your service, Sir. That is our signature cocktail, the Snow Ball."

Cocktails

The little man waited politely until I finished the drink, took back the glass and gestured for me to follow him.

"Come this way, Sir."

He turned, walked over the edge of the plateau, and disappeared from sight. I stood still for a moment. I knew hallucinations could occur at altitude. I shook my head and walked to the point where he had vanished, sure that I would see nothing but the falling snow.

He was standing in front of a bright pink door, above which multi-coloured lights were flashing. I closed my eyes, stood still, waited, and then opened them again. The little man was still there, waiting patiently, and so was the door, with its lights still flashing brightly. It was just a door. On either side of it I could see the snow falling.

"Won't you come in, Sir? You'll find it to be much warmer inside."

He opened the door and ushered me through. For a moment I was still in the snow, then I heard the soft thud of the door closing behind me, the air on my facemask was warm and my snow goggles steamed over. I took them off and found myself looking into a long room lit with soft pink lighting. Long drapes of red and gold hung from a ceiling somewhere high above, and my crampons sank deeply into a dark red carpet. Ninety-twenties Chicago jazz was playing softly in the background. I gazed around me and stared in disbelief.

A hand touched my arm.

"Take your oxygen cylinder and crampons off and sit down, Sir. You've had a long trek. Another Snow Ball, perhaps?"

I took a full glass from the tray, sank into deep armchair and sipped the drink slowly, trying to make sense of it all.

"Something to eat, Sir? How about an ice cream? We've got plenty of ice cream. Actually it doesn't seem to go all that well up here. Or a Cornish pasty? We do a good Cornish pasty. Mister Mallory enjoyed our first one."

"Mallory! George Mallory? He was here?"

"Oh yes, sir, him and Mr Irvine. Nice chaps. Bit old fashioned, though. But you Sir, I think I know what you'd really enjoy. Let me get Gabriella to take care of you."

Across the room came one of the most beautiful women I had ever seen. She was tall and slim, clad in a short white toga, held by a gold pin

Cocktails

at her shoulder. Her white teeth flashed in a smile as she stretched out her hand.

"Come with me, Jim."

Her voice was soft and melodious. I took her hand, rose from the chair and stumbled along behind her. "Here we are."

Somehow we had arrived in room containing a large, circular pool filled with blue water. Tendrils of steam rose were rising, soapy bubbles danced on the surface and the scent of jasmine filled the air.

"Sit down."

By now I had given up any attempt at cogent thought. I sank down onto one of the huge sofas that surrounded the pool. She knelt in front of me, unlaced my heavy boots, took them off and rolled away my thick wool socks.

"Stand up."

She pulled me to my feet and moved around me, unzipping and sliding away layers of protective clothing, until I stood naked. "Time for nice hot bath, Jim."

I stepped into the pool and lowered myself slowly into the steaming water, stretching and luxuriating as the heat spread through my body. She looked down at me, fixing her blue eyes on mine as her hand moved to the gold pin and smiling as she pulled it free. The flimsy garment dropped to the floor, revealing a perfect naked body. Her skin was smooth and tanned golden brown, and the ends of her long blonde hair tickled the rosy pink nipples of a pair of firm full breasts. She swept her hair up behind her head and fixed it in place with the pin, stepped into the water and slipped down beside me. The golden down between her thighs glistened and soap bubbles formed rainbows between her breasts.

 She moved around until she was facing me and eased herself closer, sliding her long legs underneath mine. From somewhere she took a soft flannel and a bar of soap and, leaning forward until her nipples grazed my chest, reached around me to wash my back. Then she leaned back and washed my face, shoulders and arms.

Keeping her eyes fixed on mine, she pulled me towards her so my lower body lifted out of the water. Slowly, she soaped my chest and then worked the flannel down my stomach to my thighs. My cock was lying

Cocktails

semi-flaccid and she ran the flannel up and down its length. I groaned and she smiled, slid her fingers under the shaft, and lifted it. The flesh grew quickly into a stiff rod in her hand and she stroked it with soft, expert fingers. A long fingernail tickled the sensitive flesh, and then I lay back and groaned as her lips engulfed the head and moved down the shaft.

Her head moved slowly up and down while I soaked up the bliss of the hot water and the exquisite feeling of her lips and tongue. Far too soon she lifted her head.

"Come, Jim."

I opened my eyes and she stood, reaching out a hand to help me to my feet. We stepped out of the bath on to the thick carpet and she sank down, pulling me with her and fixing her lips on mine. We kissed, and then she pushed my head down to her breasts. I sucked first one nipple and then the other, feeling them hardening under my lips. She guided my hand between her legs and gasped with pleasure when my fingertip tickled the hard bud of her clitoris, while her fingers worked their wicked dance on my rigid cock.

We played with each other for a short time, and then she pulled me on top of her, her long slender legs splaying apart. "Now, Jim." Her voice was husky. "I want you inside me."

The sensation as I slid slowly into the hot, tight velvety tunnel between her thighs was like nothing I had ever experienced before. She wrapped her legs around me, sighing with pleasure as I closed my eyes and began to thrust. I felt like a balloon being blown up to bursting point as I fought to delay the inevitable. Slowly the delicious feeling grew stronger and stronger until I felt I could contain it no longer…

…"Goodbye, Sir."

My eyes flew open. I was dressed in my climbing gear, standing on the plateau, with the snow falling around me. The small figure in the tuxedo bowed courteously to me.

"I hope you enjoyed our service, Sir."

I gaped at him.

"Er, yes ... but how ... who are you? How come no one has ever told me about you?"

My questions tailed off, and I stood looking at his diminutive figure,

Cocktails

which was fading and vanishing behind the thickening curtain of snow. "Well, bless you, Sir," he said. "No one could have."
His voice was faint, and I had to strain to hear his final words "Our service is only here for the ones who don't survive. Goodbye, Sir."

Jim Baker is a recycled, retired Pom who has made Perth WA his home after spending his working life as an expatriate living in Canada, South America and Asia. He has been writing short stories, poetry and travel articles since retiring. Besides writing Jim spends his time walking in the Australian bush, the UK countryside and the Himalayas. Most of his stories relate to life in the different cultures that he has encountered during his travels. Jim has previously been published in the Stringybark anthologies Stew and Sinkers *and* Valentine's Day.

After Dark
— Claire Martijn

The taxi rolled away leaving her standing on the cobblestone street after dark. Streetlights were far and few. Windows of apartments all closed up against the crisp night chill. Tucking her wallet away she dug around in another pocket of her handbag extracting a set of keys that tinkled softly. Inserting a key in the lock of the door where she stood, she pushed against its heaviness, managing to prop it open as she pulled her luggage into the empty foyer. Quietly she shut the door, checking that it was latched securely then she slowly went up the stairs, lifting her luggage step by step, wincing at any sound she made. She passed one door and headed further up the narrow staircase, following its semi spiral around. The stairs ended abruptly at a door and here she held tight her luggage as she inserted another key, twisted and pushed the door inwards. It opened silently and she entered, shuffling around in the confined space. Closed and locked the door, then shrugged off her jacket, hanging it on the rack alongside a collection of other larger jackets and coats. She looked at her luggage, at the next set of stairs and decided not to try to navigate them in the inky blackness. Keeping the light off was an intrinsic aspect of her plan. She slipped out of her knee high boots, leaving them and inched her way upward. Her stockinged feet whispered over the smooth wooden boards.

A nightlight cast a muted glow at the top of the stairs, the area was large and open plan. Kitchen/dining merged with the living space. Everything was quiet. She rounded the banister and eased herself further upward into the sleeping loft.

She could hear his breathing. Soft, rhythmic, deep. The pale shape of the bed covers was before her. Placing her handbag on top of the long low set of drawers, she quickly shimmied out of her short denim skirt, pulled the lightweight jumper up over her head and tiptoed to the bed. She stopped at the skylight window and pulled back the blind, a crescent moon and bright stars shone, casting a silvery hue over the room. Undoing her bra she smiled indulgently as she now could see the bed's occupant's head nestled amongst pillows and linen. Her panties and

Cocktails

stockings quickly joined her bra on the bare floor.

Standing naked by the bed she gazed longingly down at her lover's face. No lines of worry, no tension, no frowns, or stress to be seen. But also no smiles, no eyes twinkling, no great burst of laughter. She shivered in the cool air, bent and slipped ever so quietly under the covers and eased herself close to his long warm body, holding herself mere inches away. His heat radiated and immediately her body relaxed. She wanted to touch him. Ached to trail her fingers along his hip, his thigh. Kiss his shoulder his collar bone. Feel the length of his body against hers. Hold him and caress him, wake him with nibbles, licks and sucking on his nipples. She knew that would rouse him. She knew if she kissed the skin beneath his ear, ran a hand up his inner thigh he would stir. If she kissed his lips his mouth would open and their tongues would sweep, twist and dance. He would groan and turn toward her, his legs would spread slightly, arms reach for her and drag her into his strong embrace. She would come to be lying full length upon him, his already hard cock pressed up against her belly. His hands would roam over and down her back, moulding her to him and she would melt. His hands would grab her arse.

But she held herself back. She wanted to watch him. Drink in the sight of him. Revel in the sheer delight of being near him.

He rolled further toward her, murmured something unintelligible and frowned. His arm moved and touched her stomach, paused then pushed against her. She held her ground and bit her lip to stop from giggling. He most likely would not wake properly. He was a deep sleeper. His arm moved more caught now hard up against her soft body. Frowning, eyes still firmly closed he murmured more words.

"What's that, Babe?" she whispered close to his ear. "What did you say?"

He mumbled and turned more, the arm furthest away now reaching for her, pulling her close.

"What's wrong my love?"

"Are you real?" he slurred sleepily.

She kissed his chin, his neck. "Do you want me to be real?"

"Mmm," he murmured. "Yes. Real, not a dream. Please not a dream." His arms tightened around her.

Cocktails

She licked the base of his neck, one of her hands resting on his chest, over his nipple, the other slipping lightly down his side over his hip to squeeze his arse. He pushed himself against her. His cock rigid and definitely making its presence known.

She flicked his nipple and ran feather light kisses up his neck to his jaw. He murmured appreciatively. She tugged at his lower lip with her teeth and slid the tip of her tongue inside his mouth.

He responded immediately and kissed her back almost hungrily. His arms tightened around her. Their tongues entwined. They ravished and plundered each others mouths. She melted against him. Her legs twisted around his. Their bodies fused as close as possible without any penetration.

He groaned. Hands caressing, moulding her, feeling every bare inch of her back. His eyes were still closed. The look on his face one of bliss.

She pulled away, ignored his protesting moans and kissed her way down to his chest. Her mouth found one nipple and grazed it with her teeth. He twitched. She pulled at the other with nimble fingers. He jerked, tossed his head and panted in pleasure.

His hands grabbed her arse and push her hips against his. Ground them together. He was rock hard and she was wet. But she wasn't ready to capitulate yet.

Still lower she slid, trailed hot kisses along his fevered abdomen, licked his navel, leaving one hand to trace enticing circles around one then the other nipple, pull, flick and play with them as she willed.

His cock thrust up under her chin. She ducked her head and blew softly across its tip and ever so slowly ran the tip of her tongue around its head, his foreskin completely retracted, the angry red head bobbed and his hips moved upward. She grinned, glanced up through her lashes to check his face. Still his eyes remained closed. His mouth hung open, head tossed back slightly, one of his own hands gently caressed her head, the other paid homage to the nipple that she did not. She licked her lips and bent to her task.

He cried out as first her lips then her hot moist mouth took him in. Her tongue swished and swirled. She halted as his hips moved. Allowing him time to settle, then she continued. Sucked him in, grazed her teeth under and down that sensitive skin. Pulled up, heard him catch his breath as she twisted and moved back down licking and sucking.

Cocktails

She loved his cock. Loved the delicious way it tasted. Loved the way he groaned and moaned. She kept her ministrations going and added to his heightening pleasure by cupping his heavy tight balls. The skin was puckered and leathery. He grunted as she squeezed. Called out to her as she pulled. Writhed as she sucked a bit harder. His back started to arch, his head tossed and he gasped. Both his hands clutched at her head, gentle, not daring to break the spell of her motions. He panted, called her name again. His hips started to thrust, jerk. His legs stiffened. His shoulders pressed back deep into the comforting confines of the bedding. Her mouth was wet, hot, slick and ever so skilled bringing him higher, he teetered. Her tongue flicked down and around and he shouted.

His eyes shot open. Wide. He lay gasping for air. Tangled in sweat drenched sheets. A sticky warm feeling pooling over his belly.

His arms searched the bed, hands groping. He sat up. Looked around the darkness. Where was she? The bed held no other warmth. The room smelt only of himself. He fell back, dejected and alone. He called her name. Looked up at the skylight, at the crescent moon. Had she been real?

Claire Martijn has always had a passion for writing. She attributes much of her inspiration these days to her handsome partner, J, whether that be stories of varied genre, poetry or in-depth outpourings of emotive thought-provoking writings or 'drivel' as she terms it. Written words vie for space in her everyday. Claire currently lives on the NSW south coast with her son and their dog.

Firefly

— Michael Wilkinson

I swing back and forth in the semi-darkness, enjoying the view below. The air is heavy with the scent of fragrant candles and sex. Today I chose jasmine candles. I find that it blends beautifully with the fragrance of cum. Over in the corner I spy Gemma. She appears to be on all fours with a man at both ends. The thrusting looks languid.

The piano picks up pace — James Last — and I swing a little higher. I fly up into the spotlight now and I make my signature move, spreading my legs just at the right second to illuminate the glory of my vulva to those watching from the gallery. I have asked Mark to use a pink suffused spot, so that my colour is enhanced, rather than washed out. His preference is to use white spots, with me making up for the wash out with lipstick accentuating my lips. Normally, I would agree but tonight is special and I like the colour pink. It's the colour of sex. My vulva looks like a firefly against the dark ceiling.

The club has been open for two years now. Two years, oh how they have flown — figuratively and literally. I laugh to myself as I push myself higher into the air, the wind cooling the moisture between my legs. Two years ago I was a failed ballerina, a foot injury destroying fifteen years of hard work. Today, I am queen of my eyrie, a millionaire and a purveyor of pleasure.

One hundred and one members we have and I selected each and every one of them. Men and women of all colours, ages and creeds. Our only bond, an adoration of the oh-so-human need for physical intimacy. I remember the night I had the idea. My foot was tightly bound and my ballet teacher had said that after seeing the X-rays I would never dance again. Normally injured ballet students become ballet teachers, but despite my fifteen years of training I had not finished the Solo Seal and so that pathway was out.

But years of dancing had given me a deep appreciation of the human form. Male, female. It mattered not. All got me wet. Sometimes it was a bit embarrassing having damp leotards during training. But I did notice I wasn't the only one and these were the first girls I approached after my

Cocktails

accident. Gemma still is a ballet dancer and her wonderful musculature and flexibility makes her very popular with all the members.

Once Gemma was on board, she became my main recruiter. We got another two girls from the ballet school and then evened it up by approaching a few of the studs at the university basketball club. It was important that the first members were young, fit and sexy. I charged them only a nominal amount to join. Once I had a group of eight, four women and four men, I then opened it up to other members. I started by identifying academics who flirted with the students and invited them, one by one, to a club night.

We started small, renting out part of a small sandstone building in Glebe which Gemma and I decorated on the weekends. We painted the walls a sexy dark maroon and furnished the place with comfortable leather sofas and small coffee tables. Gemma choreographed the original eight members so that when the prospective new members entered, they were treated to some fabulous sex positions. Quite amazing what eight, fit, young people can do. The biggest problem, as ever, was that the men just couldn't wait. For example, Glenn, who played point guard and could play an entire game of basketball without ever coming off court, would come quite literally within three minutes after joining the girls at the club. But who could blame him?

Sophie our second recruit, was small and could put her toes in her mouth, she was so flexible. She loved rubbing her cunt all over Glenn's face and chest. Her grool was so prolific that she could make him look as through he was suffused in massage oil. Oh he smelt beautiful after she had rubbed him down. I loved licking him afterwards. He got hard, by God he got hard, but all I had to do was wrap my hands around his cock, and bang, he fired. Cum all over his hard tummy. The other blokes were just the same. Fine cocks, but no stamina. There was no way we were going to allow novocaine to be used in our Club. We weren't porn stars — just hedonists. So I simply decreed that none of the original four men were allowed to cum until at they had performed at least fifty minutes of cunnilingus, fellatio or some other oral sex act. This had a great side-effect, it made their cumming quite spectacular. All that pent up desire led to great explosions.

One time we had two new prospective members — Justine and

Cocktails

Philip. Justine worked in the Uni's fine art department and Philip was from a legal firm. Gemma invited them both to witness a Gemma choreographed gang-bang, set to Swan Lake. The finale was having the four basketballers stand in a circle around Sophie, after fifty minutes of synchronised pussy munching, and spray her with cum. Gemma had them hold each other's penises and wank themselves to a climax. They were like fire hoses. Justine signed up on the spot and Philip offered to buy a Gold membership if I could guarantee he could suck off Sophie that evening. I didn't say no, nor did Sophie.

Philip did want to finish by cumming in her cunt, but we had a strict policy that members needed to furnish a doctor's certificate on a monthly basis showing they were clean. He had to wait another week — but I think he thought it was worthwhile.

By last November, we were up to fifty members — half our target, and as planned, while their figures were no longer Venus and Adonis, the figures that they could pay were fabulous. Philip got his Gold membership for $8000 pa. By November, Gold memberships were $15,000 pa. But we did have to open four nights a week to accommodate the member's expectations.

The last twenty members had to pay $20,000 pa for their membership. I had always thought that it would be difficult to get a gender balance in our members, but I was wrong. Women were just as keen to be involved as men. Whether it was their relatively repressed childhoods being forgotten or just their desire to prove that women are the equal of men in everything, I'm not sure. But it was beautiful to see everyone so involved.

So here I am, on my swing, above the semi-darkened room below, watching the coming and parting of couples, trios, quads and quins. Some men and women simply sit in the deep couches and watch the passing parade. I like to watch too. It's quite amazing from up here — everything looks so different. Over there is Martin and Serena, with, oh, yes, Tony. Martin and Tony are true hedonists. The Attorney-General would be proud to see how they enjoy themselves. Martin is quite short and muscly while Tony is slender, tall and nearly hairless. He's a beautiful man. Martin is slowly pushing himself into Serena's pussy. From here I can see the lights reflecting off her moisture as he

Cocktails

withdraws. Tony is lying underneath Serena having his thin, lengthy cock sucked while he licks Martin's shaft. About every fifth stroke Martin withdraws completely and Tony licks him dry. I love the sensuality of it all. It so reminds me of the deliberateness of some of my old ballet dances. Controlled but slowly rising in intensity.

I feel my wetness grow as I swing back and forth, keeping my eyes firmly on Tony and Martin. I wonder which one of the three will come first. Serena is multi-orgasmic and she can go for hours, taking men and women without break. I once asked her if she used lube to keep going for such lengthy times and she looked at me with her big almond eyes and simply said, "Why, when I love it so? I am perpetually wet." I know how she feels.

This swing has liberated me from the limp caused by my shattered foot. No more hobbling like a lame duck with nobody wanting me. No, from here I fly like the birds. I have a small control box that allows me to lower myself from the ceiling down to being among the members. I can be at any level. I rather like to come down to chin height and have a man, or woman, eat me out. Once I fell off my swing I came so hard, but normally I just let them nibble, suck and lick until their jaws are tired. I get much pleasure out of that.

Or if I do feel like it I can lower myself to hip height and have a man plough into me as I gently swing to and fro on his cock. It's like milking. My pussy muscles contract and tighten to grip him and I can control him until I want him to cum. Oh the power.

Having all been tested we don't use condoms, or dental dams or any such device as we want the pure, delightful feeling of skin on skin — everywhere. The only exception is anal sex, where condoms are required. Nobody seems to mind. And our only other rule, is no drugs, other than alcohol. But nobody is to get drunk. Drunks don't know how to control themselves and for men makes them limp and useless. We need hard men, not drunk men.

I think Tony is going to come first. Martin has put a condom on and is entering Tony from behind while Serena is now sucking Tony. I don't imagine he will last long with those two working on him so well. I'm right. I smile as I see him spray over Serena. She scoops some cum up on her finger and offers it to Martin, who without hesitation licks it off. It's all very sweet and loving.

Cocktails

Our biggest expense, other than rent is keeping the leather couches and the plush carpet clean, although I suspect that semen and pussy juice keeps the leather supple. The couches are so soft.

I'd love to do the Nutcracker on our small stage, I'd probably be Clara or the Sugar Plum Fairy. I'd have Martin and Tony as gingerbread soldiers and Serena and Gemma as the mice, eating the soldiers. I put three and then four fingers inside myself and find my g-spot with the very tip of my fingers as I think of how I would have the mice go about their nibbling…

I see on my side-table my 'get well' cards and the spidery writing of my ballet teacher wishing me luck in whatever venture I try in the future. Shifting my aching foot under the bedcovers, I smile. I have it all planned out and my fingers return to my warm, wet place until the ward lights come on.

Michael Wilkinson is an Australian writer with a love of the bush. He has been writing since the age of twelve and now, three and a half decades later is still writing. He writes both fiction and non-fiction. He has been published in twelve Stringybark Stories anthologies, including the three erotic fiction collections: The Heat Wave of '76, Between the Sheets *and* Valentine's Day.

Japanese Slipper
— Jen Proctor

From the driveway of my house, I can see the back of a Japanese restaurant. It is a dark, brick structure with side walls which adjoin other shops. Railing runs along the entire length of the wall, a metre out. At the Japanese restaurant, a screen door is propped open with a chair. There a young, Asian man sits. He has high cheekbones, smooth skin and a cigarette dangling from the corner of his mouth. Wearing black pants, a black cap, and a white chef's jacket rolled up to the elbows, he is drying a silver bowl with a white and blue, striped tea towel. There are veins in his forearms and on the back of his hands. He stands, tucks the tea towel into his waistband, and disappears inside. After a moment he comes back outside, leans on the railing and continues smoking.

I walk down my driveway, lined with flowering Grevilleas, and check the mailbox. There is no mail yet. It is sunny and there are finches in the hedge. My husband would think I check the mail too often, but it is difficult to know what to do when the baby is asleep. Besides, the sunshine and the birds make me feel alive.

I look up. White clouds with dark undersides scud across the sky. Wind stirs the hedge. A storm is predicted.

The chef's face points my way but a cloud of gauzy smoke and the shade of his cap obscure his gaze.

I walk back to the house. Inside is silence, the smell of pine cleaner and the slight sweetness of milk vomit. I lock the door, go to my room and lay down on my back in the marital bed. I need sleep but the sunlight and the smell of rain has made my heart race.

Masturbation has always made me feel guilty. I should save myself for my husband. When I was young, my mother told me it was dirty to touch yourself; that nice girls didn't do it. But we were allowed to take off our clothes during thunderstorms and run around in the rain.

It is warm as bliss beneath the quilt. I arch my back and remove my bra beneath my t-shirt, pulling the straps through my sleeves one after the other. My body expands like it has been untied. I wriggle my jeans down to my knees, wet my fingers with my tongue and slide them underneath the covers.

Cocktails

The house sighs as though it's breathing. The open window rattles. A car passes and someone coughs and the bottlebrushes hiss in the wind. I close my eyes.

"Hello," says someone with a Japanese accent. The chef stands over me. His hair is dark brown and very fine, his hat gone. He takes the corner of my quilt and lifts it back. He raises his eyebrows. Slowly, heart pounding like rain on corrugated iron, I take my hand away. He laughs without sound, though I feel a pressure; a humid breeze. Letting go the bedding, he pushes my shirt up beneath my chin and gazes at my bare breasts.

A gust of wind climbs the outer wall and slides through the window, across my body, prickling my skin. The man leans down and touches both of my breasts softly with his hands like he knows them: owns them. The nipples grow hard against his palms. He leans down, kisses one and presses his lips closed around the bud.

The man slides two fingers into his mouth, pulls them out, reaches down and pushes his fist between my thighs. He watches my face. Smirking, he pushes inside my opening.

Wetness wells, muscles melt. I tilt my pelvis, welcoming him, but my jeans prevent me from opening my legs. Fingers thrust inside me; once, twice, more, harder, faster. My breathing quickens.

The man slides his fingers from me, straightens. He is tall for a Japanese man — maybe five ten. He rubs the slippery tips of his fingers together, considers them a moment and then leans down until his lips are beside my ear.

"*I want to fuck you*," he whispers.

I lay still, hardly breathing, eyes closed. He grabs my jeans cuffs and pulls them down, off my legs. He grasps my ankles, pulls them apart. I listen for the swish and slide sounds of undressing. I imagine his ruffled hair, smooth chest, and small, dark nipples.

I stare as the man slides his pants down to his ankles. He has tight planes of muscle that run down his abdomen like patterns on the bed of a dry river. His erection is dark russet against his pale thigh. Slowly, he climbs between my open legs on knuckles and knees. He nudges them further apart. He reaches for my wrists, wraps his slender fingers around them and holds them above my head.

Cocktails

I turn my face to the window. A honeyeater launches from the branch of a hibiscus bush. The branch twangs and swings. The wind gushes against the side of the house. I realize that the windows are wide to the storm, the washing still on the line, linen and jumpsuits swinging in the pre-storm breeze.

My visitor waits, silent and still.

I refocus.

The erection is between my thighs, pointing towards my plum coloured sex. He smiles and lowers his hips, pushes inside my fleshy folds. I writhe beneath his weight. Taut muscle: lithe strength. The heat of his neck burns against my cheek. He thrusts inside, a sudden force, smooth and full as a Japanese Slipper.

Our breathing grows stronger as the wind throws debris against the side of the house. He pushes in; a solid tide, then out, and back in. He is rhythm; storm and sea and sweet, hard pressure.

I long to stimulate my clitoris. Climax stays just out of reach like a shy dancer at the edge of the room.

He pauses, slides out and rolls me onto my side, facing away. The bed jiggles as he nestles tight against my back and tucks his knees in behind mine, his hardness sandwiched between my right buttock and his stomach.

I hear the chirp of honeyeaters. A door slams over the road. A car rolls past and wind buffets the trees.

He moves his hips and adjusts his length along the vertical crease of my buttocks. With two hands, I reach behind and ease the plump halves apart. He slides between.

The blunt hardness nudges the firm puckering, dimples the flesh. Fingers grip my hipbones. I breathe open-mouthed and will my body to yield; to allow access.

He shoves firmly, working against the tight opening until it gives. I give a short exhalation as the ridge behind his mushroom tip pushes inside. Warm beads of moisture dapple my forehead and temples. Sweat trickles down my spine. The stretching flesh sends cold heat up my spinal cord, down the backs of my legs to the soles of my feet like the after-effect of a cocktail drunk in haste. But his insistence is rewarded by an inch of progression into the narrow passage which tingles and widens around the thick head of his penis.

Cocktails

Thunder crackles across the sky and a spear of light stretches from cloud to earth as he gives one long, hard push and slides further inside. I pitch forwards, panting and burning. The wind howls its pleasure and the rain begins to fall.

Around the rigid shaft, smooth muscles ease and soften. He pulls gently on my hips, pulling me back against him. In stages, he pushes inwards, draws out a small way, and then pushes back in until he is buried up to the wide hilt.

He lifts my upper leg and rests it into the crook of his elbow as he moves back and forth inside my body. Outside torrential rain pounds the road and grass and driveway. Without pause, he reaches over, finds the opening, and slides two fingers inside. He alternates thrusting, front and back and rubs my clitoris with the side of his thumb.

My womb, anus and stomach, clench and spasm as the wind moans. Waves of rain hammer against the north facing windows. He strains and gasps, and inside me, pulses.

I lay there in a syrupy afterglow, warm and swollen and delicious. The room hums with rain, the soft drumming of water. I imagine he showers before he leaves.

I hear the baby stir. I rise slowly, shower quickly. In the bathroom mirror, my chest and neck are rash red, my hair ruffled like bottlebrush flowers. I feel rested; liquid as honeysuckle nectar.

I pause at the window. Across the road is the Japanese chef. He is sheltering beneath a faded orange awning which stretches over the back door of the restaurant. He throws a cigarette butt down on the ground and grinds his heel. His gaze sweeps the dark sky and then the street. I wonder if he inhales the fresh, sweet-water scent that comes from the warm bitumen. As I watch, he adjusts his cap, turns and goes inside.

Jen Proctor is a freelance writer who lives in Perth with her husband, children and any native critters that happen to drop in. She has a science degree, loves chocolate mud-cake and is terrified of heights. This is her first erotic offering.

Cocktails

The Stringybark Erotic Short Fiction Award 2014

Winner
Hangman's Blood — Maria Bonar

Second Place
The Vibrator — Derek Wayne

Third Place
Make Believe — Robin Storey

Highly Commended
Snow Ball — Jim Baker
Screaming Orgasm — Maria Bonar
Dark and Stormy — Danielle Chedid
Soixante-Neuf — Julie Davies
White Russian — Julie Davies
The Buzzer — Bernadette Frances
Kiss in the Dark — Adam Ipsen
Adios Motherfucker — Michelle Irwin
Lychee Martini — Dusty Lane
Harvey Wallbanger — Meg Main
After Dark — Claire Martijn
Deep Dark Secret — Claire Martijn
No Regrets — Sorcha Ni Mhaolmhuaidh
Water from the River Ganges — Rowena Michel
In the Saddle — R.L. Phoenix
Japanese Slipper — Jen Proctor
Mermaid — Josh Redman
Hot Carl Msagro — Diana Thurbon
Dusty Rose — Shane von Liger
Firefly — Michael Wilkinson
Satin Sheets — Michael Wilkinson
Red Lotus — Samira Wyld

The Cocktails

Mermaid
1 part amaretto
1 part blue curacao
1 part gin
1/2 part Midori
1 part white rum
1 part white tequila
1 part vodka
3 splashes pineapple juice
2 splashes sour mix
1 splash lemonade

Shake ingredients in a cocktail shaker with ice. Strain into large glass. Strain nothing else.

No Regrets
1 part tequila
1 part Bailey's Irish Cream

Pour the Irish Cream into a shot glass, add the tequila, and shoot.

Dark and Stormy
2 parts dark rum
3 parts ginger beer
1/2 part of lime juice

Mix with ice. Drink very, very, carefully.

Cocktails

Deep Dark Secret
3 parts dark rum
1 part light rum
1 part Kahlua
1 part heavy cream

In a shaker half-filled with ice cubes, combine all of the ingredients. Shake well. Strain. Enjoy.

Screaming Orgasm
2 parts vodka
3 parts Bailey's Irish cream
1 part Kahlua

Pour first vodka, then Bailey's, then Kahlua into a cocktail glass over crushed ice. Stir. Drink lustily.

Make Believe
4 parts Marasquin cherry liqueur
2 parts white rum
1 part Framboise raspberry liqueur
1 part pineapple juice

Stir ingredients together in a cocktail glass over crushed ice. Garnish with a mint leaf, and serve with alacrity.

White Russian
3 parts vodka
1 ½ parts Kahlua
1 ½ parts cream

Pour the ingredients into an old-fashioned glass filled with ice. Stir well. Imbibe with enthusiasm.

Cocktails

Lychee Martini
3 parts lychee liqueur
2 parts vodka
1 dash lychee juice

Combine all ingredients in a cocktail shaker with/without ice. Shake well, strain into a cocktail glass, and serve with or without knickers.

Water from the River Ganges
2 parts vodka
1 part orange juice
4 parts cola

Add 1/4 slice lime to the bottom of a glass, along with two ice cubes. Pour the ingredients in and enjoy, while thinking of lithe young men.

Kiss in the Dark
1 part cherry brandy
1 part dry vermouth
1 part gin

Stir all ingredients with ice, strain into a cocktail glass, and serve. Applying cuffs is optional.

Cocktails

Hangman's Blood
1 part gin
1 part rum
1 part whiskey
1 part brandy
1 part port
4 parts stout beer
3 parts champagne

Add all together but there is no room for ice so chill everything beforehand. Enjoy with haggis.

Hot Carl
1 part tequila
1 part watermelon schnapps
1 ½ parts sweet and sour mix
1 part tequila

Combine all ingredients in a cocktail shaker half-filled with ice cubes. Shake well, strain into an old-fashioned glass, and serve. Leave out the zucchini.

Satin Sheets
2 parts brandy
1 part peach schnapps
1 tsp grenadine syrup
4 parts orange juice
1/2 glass ice cubes

Combine first four ingredients in a mixing glass, stir, and pour into a glass half filled with ice cubes. Do not stiry with a vibrahead as it causes the drink to go translucent.

Cocktails

Soixante-Neuf
1 part gin
4 parts champagne
1 part lemon juice

Pour the gin and lemon juice into a shaker with ice, and strain into a champagne flute. Top off the glass with champagne. Add a lemon peel twist Not to be imbibed while on the telephone.

In the Saddle
1 part bourbon
¼ part of lapsang souchong tea infused simple syrup
1/10 part of lemon juice

In a mixing glass add all ingredients with ice and shake hard for ten seconds. Strain into a cocktail glass and garnish with a lemon twist or candied lemon peel. Horseshoes are optional.

Red Lotus
1 ½ parts vodka
1 ½ parts lychee liqueur
3 parts cranberry juice
lychee fruit
1 lemon twist

Combine ingredients in a cocktail shaker with ice. Shake well and pour into the margarita glass. Garnish with a lemon twist. No need to keep your knickers on with this drink.

Cocktails

Vibrator
2 parts vodka
¾ part raspberry liqueur
Orange juice
Cranberry juice

Pour liquors into an ice-filled glass. Fill with equal parts of orange and cranberry juice. Shake, garnish with two cherries, and serve. Check your batteries regularly.

Harvey Wallbanger
3 parts vodka
6 parts orange juice
1 part Galliano
Orange slice for garnish
Maraschino cherry for garnish

Pour the vodka and orange juice into a glass with ice cubes. Add the Galliano. Garnish with the orange slice and maraschino cherry. Snakes love this drink.

Dusty Rose
2 parts cherry brandy
1 part white creme de cacao
4 parts cream

Shake (or swing on clothes line) the ingredients, pour into a cocktail glass, and serve.

Cocktails

Buzzer

2 parts whisky
1 part orange juice
1 part raspberry liqueur
1 part lemon juice
1 part lemonade

Pour the whisky, orange juice, raspberry liqueur, lemon juice and lemonade into a cocktail shaker half-filled with ice cubes. Shake well, strain into cocktail glass, and serve. Keep batteries fully charged.

Adios Motherfucker

1 part vodka
1 part rum
1 part tequila
1 part gin
1 part Blue Curacao liqueur
4 parts sweet and sour mix
4 parts lemonade

Pour all ingredients except the lemonade into a chilled glass filled with ice cubes. Top with lemonade and stir gently.

Snowball

1 part advocaat liqueur
2 parts lemonade
Ice cubes

Take the glass and rub the edge on a lemon, then dip the rim in sugar. Drop the ice cubes into the glass, pour in liqueur and fill it up with lemonade. Remove crampons. Stir.

Cocktails

After Dark
1 part Licor 43 liqueur
1 part Bailey's Irish cream
1 part Kahlua coffee liqueur

Layer, in order. Drink.

Firefly
2 parts vodka
4 parts grapefruit juice
1 part grenadine

Pour the vodka and grapefruit juice into a mixing glass with ice. Stir well. Strain into a highball glass filled with ice. Add the grenadine and allow it to float up from the bottom. Add one sugar plum fairy.

Japanese Slipper
1 part Midori melon liqueur
1 part Cointreau
1 part lime juice

Combine equal parts of each ingredient in a cocktail glass. Stir up a storm, and serve.

About the Judges

David Vernon is a full time writer and editor. While he is known for his non-fiction books about birth: *Men at Birth*, *Having a Great Birth in Australia*, *Birth Stories* and *With Women*, he has turned his hand to writing science articles for newspapers and magazines as well as scribbling the odd short story or two. He established the *Stringybark Short Story Awards* in 2010 to promote short story writing. He is currently trying to write an Australian history book. He is the Chair of the ACT Writers Centre. David's website is: www.davidvernon.net

Tessa King is a primary school teacher who spends her days teaching six year olds how to correctly structure their sentences and spell words such as clock: "Do not leave out the 'l', dear!" Tessa has lost herself in the pages of countless novels starting with *Harry Potter* and arriving at her present favourite *Daughter of Smoke and Bone*. One day when she is old and determined she will write her own novel which has been stewing in the back of her mind for the past decade. In the meantime she will paint pictures and enjoy living in country NSW.

Jamie Todling's early passions were for all things to do with shopping, writing and history, in particular, various world mythologies. Now all grown up he buys for a living and writes for a hobby, but would much prefer it to be the other way around. He is an avid reader of pretty much anything that falls in front of him and can be seen haunting the rows of shelves of bookstores and libraries fossicking for a forgotten gem. Jamie has previously judged the *Stringybark Flash and Microfiction Award 2012* and *The Stringybark Erotic Fiction Award 2013*.

Cocktails

Arna Walker is a Kiwi with a long held love of literature. She left her beloved homeland some years back to seek her fortune in Australia as an accountant. Whilst still looking for the fortune she does lots of reading, travelling to obscure parts of the globe, quilting and other crafts, and walking her dog. Arna previously judged the *Stringybark Short Story Award 2013*.

More stories please!

Feeling bereft that this book is over? You can find many more stories at the Stringybark Stories Award Website. All anthologies are for sale and are reasonably priced. Visit: www.stringybarkstories.net

Acknowledgements

A book is the creative output of many people and therefore please indulge me while I thank a few people. Firstly, thank you to the writers who have so willingly entered Stringybark competitions and thus given us an opportunity to choose their writing for publication. Secondly, I thank my family for allowing me the time to select, edit and present to you this wonderful collection of stories. Finally, thank you Aislinn Batstone for her wonderful work as a proof-reader. Any errors remaining are not Aislinn's fault but mine — or the bunyip's fault that lives in my dam.

Inspiring Creativity

More from Stringybark Publishing

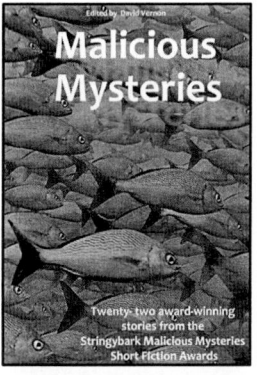

Malicious Mysteries — Twenty award-winning stories from the Stringybark Malicious Mysteries Award

Murder most foul. Ghostly images. A stumped detective. A skilled taxidermist. They are all here in this collection of malicious mysteries.

Available from www.stringybarkstories.net and all good bookshops.

Valentines Day — Twenty-three award-winning stories from the Stringybark Erotic Short Fiction Awards

These sexy tales will charm, arouse and provide warmth on the coldest evening. From the discreet to the explicit there is something for every reader.

Available from www.stringybarkstories.net and all good bookshops.

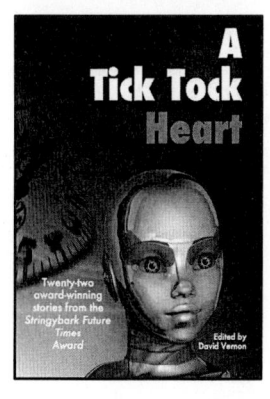

A Tick Tock Heart — Twenty-two award-winning stories from the Stringybark Future Times Awards

Be catapaulted into a future earth with these intriguing tales from Australian and international SF and Spec Fiction authors.

Available from www.stringybarkstories.net and all good bookshops.

Fight of Flight — *twenty one award-winning short stories from the Stringybark Young Adult Fiction Awards*

Showcased here are some of Australia's best YA authors. Twenty-one contemporary stories that interest today's teenagers.

Available from www.stringybarkstories.net and all good bookshops.

The Very End of the Affair — *twenty-four award-winning short stories from the Stringybark Humorous Short Fiction Awards*

These tales will make you snigger, laugh, guffaw and grin. From celebratory chefs to iGods, you'll have a wonderful time reading some great Australian humour.

Available from www.stringybarkstories.net and all good bookshops.

Side by Side — *twenty-three award-winning tales from the Stringybark Short Story Awards*

A wonderful collection of delightful and intriguing tales from Australian and international short story writers.

Available from www.stringybarkstories.net and all good bookshops.